Sundown Inheritance

To hired gun Cado Roma, it seemed like easy money volunteering for the unusual job of wet-nursing Chet Halleran, the wayward son of a rancher. But the boy was a violent brute and quickly drew Roma into a situation fraught with danger.

Not even befriending the tough town marshal could help him, as he becomes entangled in the drama of a disintegrating family. Falling for Halleran's lovely sister was a further complication!

Now it was finally time for Roma to respond in the only way he knew: with fist and gun. It would prove to be a bloody showdown.

By the same author

Rodeo Renegade
Epitaph of Vengeance
Long Ride to Green River
Railroad Law

Sundown Inheritance

TY KIRWAN

A Black Horse Western

ROBERT HALE · LONDON

© Ty Kirwan 2001
First published in Great Britain 2001

ISBN 0 7090 6926 X

Robert Hale Limited
Clerkenwell House
Clerkenwell Green
London EC1R 0HT

Typeset by
Derek Doyle & Associates, Liverpool.
Printed and bound in Great Britain by
Antony Rowe Limited, Wiltshire.

One

A slight breeze escaped as the last ray of sunlight was dragged over the horizon. Coming out of the rocky fastnesses of the Chechako Badlands, the lone rider kept his horse at walking pace. There were a few sounds around him as nocturnal creatures began their day. A coyote yipped his plaintive call to a mate who didn't reply. From the distance came a cry of pain or love, then the silence that was night flooded like a raging torrent. He was alone with only the plod of his horse's hoofs for company. The night was enormously empty, without even a voice to give life to it except his own.

He eased his weary pony up a steep grade and into a narrow defile that opened into a valley. An owl drifted down on silent wings, skimming low over him as he reined up to study the sprawling silhouette of a ranch up ahead. The dark green of the foothills behind the buildings was almost black in the deep shadows. Despite an immense weariness, he sat awhile in the saddle. Satisfied, he used a gentle prod with his heels to move the tired pony on.

The lettering Rainbow Ranch was scorched into the wood above the arch he rode through. It was a large spread. Lamplight glowed in two lower windows of the big frame house. Some broncs moved restlessly in a corral, but otherwise everything was quiet, deserted.

He dismounted at a hitching rail at the front of the house. As the door of the house opened, he quickly turned. A chunky figure carrying a rifle was back-lit in the doorway. The figure approached, a flickering lantern in one hand. Close to the new arrival, the man raised the lantern and peered into his face. Putting up a hand to shield his eyes, the rider said in a low voice,

'Either lower that light mister, or put down the rifle.'

Moving the lantern, the man showed more of himself. Middle-aged, he was solidly built. He had a ruggedness, a toughness, a general appearance of physical usefulness that would deter all but the foolhardy. He turned a name into a question. 'Cado Roma?'

When the newcomer confirmed this with a curt nod, the older man introduced himself 'I'm Hal Halleran.'

'I figured as much,' Roma said. The moon was a cold slice of light in a segment of black sky. 'You sent for me. It's been a long ride from Santa Fe.'

'It'll be worth your while, Roma. I pay top rates. I'll wake Ed Baker, my foreman, and he'll fix you up with a cot in the bunkhouse. We'll talk in the morning.'

'I'll sleep in a barn, not with your men, and we'll talk now, Halleran,' Roma said as he tied his pony to the rail.

'I ain't hired your gun as such, Roma,' Halleran half explained.

Bending under his pony, undoing the cinch, the gunman asked sharply. 'What are you trying to tell me, Halleran?'

'You'll be picking up good money whatever I want you to do.'

'Wrong, Halleran. It's me who decides whether I *want* to do something.'

'Me and the hands are leaving tomorrow with a beef shipment, Roma,' the rancher said as if that should mean something to Roma.

'I won't go on a trail drive, Halleran.'

'I ain't about to ask you to, Roma.' Halleran shifted his rifle so that it rested comfortably under his arm. 'Look, let me get you bedded down and we'll talk about this in the morning.'

'We'll talk now.'

'I'm darned if you ain't more prickly than a cactus, Roma,' Halleran complained with a gruff laugh. 'It's like this here. I got myself a hothead son named Chet. He's trouble, Roma, but his ma and me still love him. I want you to make sure he don't get into no bother while I'm away. That's what I'll be paying you for.'

Looking levelly at the rancher, Roma said, 'I hire out my gun. What you're looking for is a nursemaid.'

'My boy reached the age of twenty last branding time. I ain't looking for no nursemaid. I need a hard man like you. He's got a liking for redeye, for women, and for hell raising.'

'Why don't you take him on the drive with you?'

Halleran snorted. 'I can't risk letting that wild kid loose in Kansas City, Roma. He'll ride into Minerva Wells soon's I leave. Chet hangs around the Pleasure Palace, the worst saloon in town. It's full of hard men and harlots, Roma, and that's a mighty dangerous combination.'

'Sounds like you've got yourself a real problem, Halleran.'

'But you'll help me?' an anguished rancher asked.

Not answering, Roma pulled the saddle off his pony. 'Wake your ramrod now, Halleran, and have him get someone to take care of my horse.'

'Does that mean you're staying, Roma?'

'All it means is that I'm going to bed down here for the night. Where's this kid of yours now?'

'I got him repairing drift fences with a couple of the boys on the northern range,' the rancher replied.

'We'll talk in the morning,' Roma answered.

'I'll see that your cayuse is taken care of,' Halleran said. 'There's straw in that barn yonder. You can bed down in there.'

With a curt nod, Roma hoisted his saddle up on

his shoulder and walked away.

'Roma.' Halleran called his name sharply. The gunman stopped, waiting, but didn't turn. 'I've had 'em all pass through here in my time,' Halleran continued, 'redskins driven crazy by firewater, renegades, outlaws, mule-skinners as big as grizzlies.'

'Meaning?'

Halleran addressed Roma's back. 'Meaning that them that tried to get the better of Hal Halleran never left. I buried them up there on the hill.'

The gunslinger walked away from Halleran without uttering a single word.

Queenie Ralph turned the oil lamp down low, setting fiery worms chasing round the wick as she went to the window to pull the curtain to one side. The dull yellow cast a moving shadow on the wall as her husband moved up to peer over her shoulder.

Richard Ralph asked, 'What's happening?'

'I think that the man dad's hired to take care of Chet has just arrived,' his wife replied, an anxious expression on her face. 'I don't like the look of him, Richard.'

'I'm perfectly capable of looking after your brother, Queenie.'

Queenie made no comment. Chet got into scrapes with people capable of eating Richard alive. But she couldn't be so cruel as to tell him that. It was painful enough to see the quiet contempt her father held Ralph in. In what was a man's world, her husband was a misfit. Richard could not accept his weaknesses, so he ignored them. But then some small thing, perhaps a minor disparaging remark by her father, would provoke a storm in him.

The ideal man would be a balance between Chet and Richard, a creature with her brother's courage held in check by her husband's caution. Such a man probably didn't exist. Even her father had too much aggression, too much suppressed violence, both of which came with the territory.

By the light of her father's lantern out in the yard, she could see the hard-featured, darkly handsome stranger. He wasn't a big man, but the gun holstered low on his right hip added a frightening dimension that owed nothing to physical size. She feared for her brother. It would be dangerous for Chet should he get on the wrong side of this man.

With her father having always taken care of the myriad details that went into the daily routine of a big ranch it frightened her to think of him surrendering a certain amount of his authority to a stranger. Queenie had been happy here during the Rainbow's growth to greatness. Ed Baker, the foreman, fitted in like part of the family. The newcomer out in the yard was an unwanted intrusion.

'I promise you that I won't be far from the house while your dad is away and that man's here,' her husband said in a half whisper.

'Thank you, Richard.'

Her sarcasm had Queenie ashamed of her disloyalty. In a way, Richard deserved admiration. Having suffered from tuberculosis when young, his parents had brought Richard out West. They had opened a general store in Minerva Wells. The disease had left him physically feeble. He had been working as a teller in the bank in Minerva Wells the day an outlaw gang had looted the family store, murdering his mother and father.

When he wasn't fussing around her, pretending to be the man he never could be, Queenie would be fully aware of what it took her husband to get through each day. The catastrophe of his illness and the tragic deaths of his parents formed a cross too heavy for perhaps even the strongest of men to carry.

They jerked a little apart as the door opened and her mother came in. Like most frontier women, Muriel Halleran was old before her time. The comforts that came from a successful ranch had to be paid for in the hard currency of worry and fear. There always seemed to be some problem, some danger, some threat either actual or implied.

'What is happening, Queenie?' her mother enquired. 'I don't like your father going out there at this time of night.'

'There's nothing to worry about, Mother. He's only talking to the man who's come to keep Chet out of trouble.'

Coming to the window to look out, Muriel Halleran gave a shuddering shiver. 'Is that him?'

'That's him, Mother,' Queenie replied, anxiously adding as her mother turned quickly from the window: 'What's the matter?'

'I saw the likes of that man many times in the old days, Queenie. I do hope that your father hasn't made a mistake.'

'I think that we can safely assume that he has,' Richard Ralph muttered. 'I never thought I'd see the day when the Rainbow Ranch hired a professional gunman – a professional killer.'

'We can't say that's what he is,' an alarmed Queenie protested. Though it was plain that her husband was probably correct she didn't want to believe it.

'One look at that fellow is enough, Queenie.'

'I'm afraid that I agree with Richard, dear,' Muriel Halleran said. 'But maybe that man is exactly what we need to save your brother from harm while your father is away on the drive. We must pray that this man of Hal's can keep Chet under control.'

'Really, Mother!' Queenie sounded a little scornful. 'Can you honestly imagine that Chet will put up with somebody acting as a wet-nurse for him? He'll wait until that man turns his back, then he'll sneak off and ride into town as fast as he can.'

'If he does, then I fear that one night he won't come home,' Muriel Halleran remarked sorrowfully.

'Shhh!' Queenie dropped the curtain back into place. 'Father's coming back in.'

*

Hal Halleran walked slowly up the steps on to the veranda, chin resting on his chest, deep in thought. The only problem he had with Cado Roma was whether the gunfighter would take on the job of guarding his son. Roma's reputation had spread far and wide. In the light of the lantern, Halleran had seen the coldness in his eyes, eyes that were faded, with distance in them. Not for one moment did he underestimate the deadliness of this taciturn man.

He accidentally caught the stock of his rifle against the doorjamb as he came into the room. Halleran saw how the crack it made had startled his wife, daughter, and son-in-law. Then he realized that it had made him jump, too. All of them were in a nervous state, and it was all down to Chet. The antics of his son had got them so they no longer wondered *if* something terrible would happen to him, but *when*. Dropping his hat on a mohair sofa, he ran quick fingers through his thinning grey hair.

Thoughts of his son and the sight of his son-in-law brought an instant depression to Hal Halleran. He had started the Rainbow with a herd of fifty scraggly cows and a quarter-section of land. Now he had a cattle company that dominated the region. Good fortune had played a big part in his success, but where was his luck now? The Rainbow Ranch represented a lifetime's hard work, but it was something that must go on when that lifetime came to an end. His son wasn't capable of running the business now and, much as he loved the boy, Halleran doubted that he ever would be. His daughter was a bright, intelligent woman with a thick seam of Halleran grit running through her. But she wasn't a man; neither, sadly, was her husband.

'Who is that stranger, Pa?' Queenie asked, going to the lamp to turn up the wick. Golden light brought the room back to life, spilling against the lace-curtained windows and making a pattern out in the yard.

'His name's Cado Roma.' Hal Halleran said.

'A gunman?' Richard Ralph asked, a tremor in his high voice, as ever when he spoke to his domineering father-in-law.

Halleran let the expression on his face serve as an answer, and his wife's paled as she said, 'Do we really need that sort of person, Hal?'

'Perhaps not, Muriel. Maybe I should have taken on a bank clerk.'

The barbed remark was intended to hurt Richard Ralph. Halleran was gratified when he saw his son-in-law flinch, and despised the younger man even more because of his reaction. He had the power to play on Ralph, to hurt, goad, sting, irritate or humiliate him.

'It occurred to me, Pa,' Queenie began, 'that this Somer—'

'Roma,' Halleran corrected her.

'This Roma might well cause even more trouble than Chet.' Queenie looked at her husband, trying to measure something of his hurt in his thin, tight face.

Shaking his head to cancel out what his daughter had said, Halleran explained. 'Cado Roma will be on the Rainbow payroll, so he'll do exactly what's asked of him.'

'You mean that you'd put your trust in a hired gun?' Queenie asked, incensed by her father's complete lack of faith in her husband.

'It's because he's a hired gun that I do trust him,' Halleran countered. 'He's here to do a job, not fool around. Ask yourselves where Chet will be, unless someone takes charge of him, this time tomorrow night.'

Queenie had a mental picture of her brother lying in bed with a horde of painted saloon girls fluttering around him. She put the image from her mind, reddening a little.

'You know best, Pa.'

Facing his daughter, the girl he used to bring candy back from town for, but now a confident young woman, Halleran suddenly felt old, unsure of himself, and vulnerable. What was a new and unsettling experience quickly passed, and he announced, 'I've a hard day ahead of me tomorrow, so I'm going to get me some sleep.'

Muriel Halleran picked up her folded pinafore from the sofa. 'I'll make us all a drink.'

Roma opened his eyes to the dull sunshine coming in through the partly open barn door and the misshapen gaps in the walls. Something other than sunlight had woken him. He checked that his rolled up gunbelt was on the straw beside him,

the handle of the Colt.45 turned his way for easy
reach. Lying still, he waited. Everything seemed
to be waiting, everywhere. Alertness was a very
special thing to a man whose life depended
entirely on his instincts and his reflexes. A
moving shadow in the doorway had him reach to
slide his gun from its holster. Roma waited, ready
to fire if threatened, prepared to hide the Colt if
not.

A medium-sized dog came slowly in through
the door. White with black spots, it sniffed around,
then stiffened as it sensed his presence. Stopping,
the animal bared its teeth at him in a silent snarl.

'Kalin.'

The dog abandoned its menacing stance as a
woman's voice called the name from outside. It
turned its head towards the doorway, tail
wagging. A young woman, obviously expecting the
barn to be unoccupied, came in and caught hold of
the dog by the long hair at the back of its neck.
'Come on, Kalin, what's the matter with you this
morning,' she was saying, before giving a startled
little jump as she suddenly became aware of
Roma lying on the straw.

'Don't be frightened, ma'am,' Roma said quietly
to ease her obvious shock.

But she was made of stern stuff and swiftly
recovered her composure. The girl was fairly tall
even in moccasins. Her hair was loosely arranged
and flamed over her shoulders as, unafraid, she
moved, passing through arrows of sunlight. Away
from him she seemed almost blonde but the shade

richened to sienna as she came nearer to him. Her free-fitting tan dress was almost the colour of her skin. A full figure made her look soft and yielding, but Roma could detect her strength and firmness.

'You're Roma,' the girl said as if telling him something that he didn't know.

'That is correct, ma'am. How do you know my name?'

'I'm Queenie Halleran ... well, Queenie Ralph now. Chet's sister.'

Standing, stretching, arms above his head, Roma said, 'Ah, the wayward son.'

'Are you going to work for my father?' she asked directly.

Taking the makings from his shirt pocket, Roma took time out to roll a cigarette. Ten minutes previously, he would not have had an answer. But, on waking, necessity had pressured him into making a decision. Before leaving Santa Fe he had lost everything but his horse, saddle, and the clothes he had on, in a game of stud poker. With no liking for the job Halleran offered, he could not afford to turn it down.

He gave a nod as he struck a match to light his cigarette. 'Yes, I guess that I'll be taking care of your little brother, ma'am.'

'He's not so little,' she told him in what sounded like a warning. 'I can't pretend to have any liking for your kind, Roma, but do you know what you're getting yourself into?'

'Sounds simple enough on the face of it, ma'am. Riding herd on a kid with a big mouth who's liable to get himself shot.'

'As you say, on the face of it,' she agreed, her eyes sliding up to meet his again. 'Didn't my father say anything else? Didn't he mention what happened with Chet the last time he went on a drive? He didn't tell you about Obadiah, Shem and Eli Slade?'

'Who are they?'

'A wild bunch, Roma. They own the Three Forks ranch on the other side of town. There used to be four of them. Noah's dead. The last time my father was away, my brother shot Noah Slade dead in the Pleasure Palace.'

A faint premonition came to Cado Roma, suggesting that Halleran would have to pay dear for what he wanted him to do. He said, 'I didn't realize that your brother was quick on the draw.'

'He is,' Queenie sighed. 'But, anyway, both of them were drunk, Noah more than Chet, which is why Chet came out of it alive.'

'And I guess . . .' Roma began but Queenie interrupted. Her lips curled full and wet. There were marks on her lower lip where she had bitten into it.

'You know the law of the West, Roma. The other three brothers have sworn to get my brother.'

'I sure hope your father was going to tell me that,' Roma muttered as the dog came alert and then a dry, hard cough came from outside.

A thin man cautiously entered the barn. Placing a possessive arm round the woman's shoulders, he said, 'Here you are, Queenie. I've been looking for you. Chet hasn't come back, and your father's worried.' He looked at Roma. 'Are you Cado Roma?'

Queenie made a hurried introduction. 'Roma, this is my husband, Richard Ralph.'

'What do you want with me, Ralph?'

'It's Mr Halleran. They're all ready to move out, but he needs to see you because he wants you to ride out to the northern range to find Chet.'

TWO

The Halleran line shack was at the furthermost
point of Rainbow land. Roma approached bluffs
making a barrier that was deceiving, for they
were cut by a score of twisting, narrow canyons.
Beyond the bluffs was a wild unsettled country
that Halleran told him had once been tenanted by
hard-riding, close-lipped men who had taken
Rainbow beef on quick raids.

That problem had long ago been settled. Chet
Halleran was now the difficulty. Hal Halleran had
agreed to the financial terms demanded by Roma,
who had then ridden out in search of Chet. He
estimated that he would arrive at the line shack
with about an hour of light left.

He had made good time. There were three
hours to go before dark when he saw the shack.
An open-fronted shed that was a long extension of
the cabin, contained only a few bags of feed. Wire
strung off the shed looped round two small pines,
growing close together, to form a corral. In it were

two shaggy, mouse-coloured mustangs.

Riding up and dismounting, Roma noticed that two saddles hung on the sawbuck. Everything so far added up to just two. But there should be three including Chet. The young Halleran may have left, but where were the remaining two line riders? There was no sign of life. Roma slid his rifle from its saddle scabbard. Keeping tight to the shed, he made it to the cabin door. Easing the door open with his foot, Roma cautiously peered inside. It was a one-room shack, built strong and snug, chinked against the winds of winter. A single bunk was on his left, and a double-decker bunk was built against the wall to his right. All three bunks had tick mattresses.

The hut was unoccupied. Roma stepped inside. The wood box behind a small cook-stove was empty, but a wall cupboard held a few dishes and canned goods. The line shack looked lived in. Opening the rear door, he found that it led first to a woodshed and then a spring under a rock ledge.

He stepped out to glance along the low, rock-veined ridge that made a barrier behind the shack. From the corner of his eye, he glimpsed a movement up on the ridge. Seeing him ride up, the two Rainbow men must have taken to the ridge to wait him out.

Inside the shack, Roma closed the door. Waiting a few seconds, he yanked the door open and stepped quickly out, rifle going up to his shoulder. He surprised two men standing up on the ridge.

They had obviously been lying prone on the edge
of the rocky ledge, watching him. The pair raised
their hands.

Roma called. 'Keep your hands up and come on
down.'

Cool, purple shadows had crept across the
lower flats now, and the bluffs behind the
approaching figures were golden in the slanting
rays of a setting sun. The two Rainbow riders
came closer and he could see that one was a
stocky, round-faced young man. With an obviously
genial manner, he was the easy-going type that
wouldn't cause any trouble unless extremely
provoked. The second man was older, leaner,
taller, and red-headed, and was the forever-
anonymous kid of person who made little or no
impression on an observer. Both of the men wore
guns bolstered high up cowboy fashion, a way that
cancelled out any chance of a fast draw.

Lowering his rifle, he said, 'Take it easy, boys.
I'm new at the Rainbow Ranch, and Halleran sent
me out to fetch his boy, Chet.'

Both showed their relief. The young puncher
gave Roma a twitchy grin, and said, 'I'm Danny
Reader, and this here's Jack Gaylor.' The older
man gave a curt nod as he warily eyed Roma.

'I'm Cado Roma. You can put down your hands,
boys. Let's go into the shack and you can tell me
about Chet.'

'There ain't a lot we can tell, Roma.' Gaylor
shook his head sadly. 'Hal told us to make sure
Chet stayed riding line with us, but you cain't tie

a bobcat down with a piece of string. He just took off hours ago.'

'Neither me nor Jack was about to stop him,' Reader said.

'Chet's plumb crazy,' Gaylor complained.

Reader gathered up an armful of wood as they went into the shack, and knelt beside the stove. Gaylor was taking coffee and three tin mugs from the wall cupboard as Roma propped his rifle in a corner and asked,

'Do you reckon the kid's gone into town?'

'He sure ain't the type to take to the hills as a hermit,' Gaylor grunted.

'Well, I guess that I'll bed down here tonight,' Roma said.

'You to round up the Halleran boy?' an incredulous Gaylor asked.

'That's what Halleran's paying me for, Gaylor.'

With a neat halo of smoke curling round his head, Danny Reader looked up from his task to advise Roma. 'If'n I were you, Roma, I'd just ride on through Minerva Wells and get myself a safer job somewhere, like trying to milk a bull buffalo.'

'That's the best advice you'll get this side of Albuquerque, Roma,' Gaylor added.

With an enthusiastic nod of agreement, Reader said, 'Chet's ten times as strong as most men. One time, me'n Jack saw him lay out three giant mule-skinners in the Pleasure Palace.'

'All the boys make sure they stay on the right side of Chet,' Gaylor explained. 'Only old Halleran ain't given up on his boy yet. He still reckons that

Chet'll settle down one day and take over running the ranch.'

'That will never happen.' Reader gestured with his head to the single bunk. 'You can bed down there for the night, Roma. Which way do you reckon on heading in the morning?'

'Into town to bring the Halleran boy back to the ranch,' Roma replied coolly.

It was close to noon when Queenie and Richard Ralph came into Minerva Wells, sitting side by side up high on the seat of a wagon. At Trail Street they took the right turn into the poplar-lined road to the store. The speed at which Minerva Wells had grown from a half-dozen shacks meant that it hadn't shaped up the way that a town should. There was no segregation between the classes. The properties of the respectable wealthy were sprinkled among the saloons of the lawless low-lifes. It would have been a design for disaster without the steel nerves and fast hands of Vern Graff, the town marshal.

The Pleasure Palace stood alone on the rise above a creek that meandered in a misshapen half-circle behind the town. It was the only one of four saloons that offered girls and entertainment. It was an architecturally ugly building that announced its unrestrained bawdiness through its garish red-and-yellow exterior decor. Inside there was a dance-bar and gambling-hall. 'Big Maxie' Howland, the owner of the saloon, did things in a grandiose way, and was inhibited only by the town marshal's strict rules.

As the Ralphs neared the Pleasure Palace, Marshal Graff came out of the courthouse and stood under the portico to light a cigar. His eyes were on the approaching wagon, and both Queenie and Richard Ralph knew that this was no accidental meeting. Richard reined up the team, and Vern Graff walked to stand and look up at Queenie.

On the south side of forty, Graff had a broken nose and his face was slightly askew, as if it had received a heavy blow at some time from which it had never recovered. This crookedness of features somehow added to a deceptively sleepy appearance that had fooled several strangers in town, to their cost.

'Your brother is here in town, Queenie,' the marshal announced conversationally.

'Oh, no!' Queenie gasped, her face whitening. 'When did he get here, Vern?'

'Last evening. He's been holed up in the Pleasure Palace ever since. He's as drunk as a hiccuping coyote right now. The whole town's been on edge in case the Slade boys ride in.'

'Couldn't you lock him up for his own good, Marshal?' an anxious Queenie asked.

'I could find an excuse to do so, Queenie,' Graff replied, 'but I can't risk the safety of other folk in town. The way Chet is he could start blasting as soon as I walked into the saloon.'

'I know how Chet is,' Queenie solemnly agreed,

then, as her husband passed her the reins, she asked, 'What's going on, Richard?'

Climbing down off the wagon, Richard Ralph answered with: 'This sort of thing can't be tolerated any longer, Queenie. You take the wagon on up to the store. I'll bring Chet along, and we'll take him home with us.'

It sounded beautifully simple, an easy solution to the whole problem. But it was nothing of the sort. Chet Halleran despised his brother-in-law when sober. In a drunken state, Chet would react violently to any attempt by Richard to interfere in his wild way of life. Richard was certainly no match for the powerfully built Chet.

'Richard!' she vainly called to her husband. 'Stop him, Vern, please.'

'I've got to stay here, keeping watch on Trail Street in case the Slades ride in,' the marshal explained. 'You take the wagon on up to the store like Richard said. If I hear anything from inside the saloon, then I'll do what I can.'

'It will be too late then, Vern.'

All the marshal could do was shrug and slap one of the greys on the flank. The wagon creaked into motion, with an ashen-faced Queenie Ralph sitting rigidly up on the seat.

Both Danny Reader and Jack Gaylor had proved to be good company. They had left with Roma before daylight. A line of pale light had run along the eastern horizon. It had been chilly before daylight had seeped through distant clouds and the sun's rays had spilled over them, turning the clouds pink. Having the two line riders guide him part of the way back from the shack had shortened Cado Roma's ride to town. They had parted on the edge of a big draw. It was an old scar deep in the land worn down by run-offs from the rains of countless springs.

Danny Reader had been riding ahead, and he reined up. 'This is where we go our different ways, pardner,' he had said, pointing ahead. 'In bad weather, Rainbow beef shelter there along the lee side of the canyon towards the cliffs.'

'Don't the cattle drift on through the canyon into that wild country beyond?' Roma asked.

'There's a three-stranded fence been strung just inside the canyon at the far end. That's your shortest way into town, Cado,' Jack Gaylor told Roma.

'If a cow can't get through, then neither can my horse,' Ramo had logically pointed out.

'Hold it right there, pard,' Reader said, dismounting to take a small roll of wire and a pair of cutters from his saddle-bag. 'Take these with you, Cado. Cut the fence to let your bronc through, then put her back together again.'

As they parted, Danny Reader had given him some last minute advice. 'If you get any problems with Chet Halleran, pard, shoot the sidewinder.'

'His old man isn't paying me to kill the boy, Danny.'

'You'd be doing everyone a good turn, including Hal Halleran.'

The good-natured Reader's opinion of Chet
Halleran had been on Roma's mind throughout
his ride to town. He had thought hard about it
while cutting the wire fence, bringing his pony
through, then carrying out the repair. Hal
Halleran was a belligerent old cuss, but a
straight, honest man and his attractive daughter
had the same kind of candid manner. Conversely,
when a family had a black sheep, then the odd one
out was usually rotten to the core. From what
Roma had heard, that seemed to be true in the
Halleran case.

As he rode into Minerva Wells, Roma was still
wondering whether he had made a mistake in
hiring out to Halleran. Reaching the end of a
crooked creek and the start of the main street, he
passed two saloons that were plainly 'blind
tigers', strictly drinking places; no girls, no
gambling. Fooled by the transplanted poplars
flanking the road, he didn't at first notice the
Pleasure Palace just up ahead. Seeing a man with
a silver star pinned to his chest, walking out from
the shade of a courthouse towards him, Roma
stopped his horse. He sat in the saddle holding
the reins in his left hand, relaxed and ready for
anything.

The interior of the saloon was confusing for
Richard Ralph. It was a long time since he'd been
in the Pleasure Palace, and then it had been at
night. There had been a natural feel to the place
then, with lights burning, heavy red drapes at the

windows, and a rowdy, boisterous crowd. Now
with just a few people present, two of them girls
who were bored and listless at a time of day when
there was no money to be made, the ambience was
all wrong. Sunlight came through the door behind
him to throw irregular patterns of light and
shadow across the floor, further disorienting him.
For some odd reason in the meagrely patronized
saloon, a narrow-shouldered man in a striped silk
shirt was playing a Hamlin organ. Inappropriate
soft dreamy music sifted over the large room.

Conscious of the increasing throbbing in his
head, Ralph's glance took in the entire room. The
saloonkeeper, 'Big Maxie' Howland, his once
powerful physique now running to fat, was
resplendent as always in a plaid waistcoat, doe-
skin trousers, and ruffled white shirt. He was
standing at his usual vantage-point from where
he could watch over every inch of his domain. A
small, limping man was sweeping the floor, his
wooden leg thumping hollowly on the planks as
he moved. Ralph saw Chet Halleran perched on a
high stool at the far end of the bar. The rancher's
son had his arms folded on the top of the bar, with
his head resting on them. There was less than
thirty feet between Halleran and himself. To
Richard Ralph this short distance was a yawning
abyss that he feared to cross. He was starkly
aware that the task ahead of him was one for
which he was poorly equipped. It was worse than
that. He was completely out of his depth.

Inhaling deeply, he hoped that some kind of

support, perhaps even an inkling of a strategy, would flow in on the air. It didn't. Ralph started across the room, skirting the card tables. At the bar he ordered a whiskey. The potency of the drink stirred his blood and he seemed to gain something from it.

Further down the bar, Chet hadn't stirred and was still unaware of his presence. A thin girl with wheat-coloured hair worn long and tied with a red ribbon at the nape of her neck, straightened up from where she had been looking over the shoulder of the man playing the organ. Coming to Ralph's side she placed a hand on his arm.

'Hello. You going to buy me a drink, mister?'

Looking at a girl who had never known a genuine friendship, Richard Ralph was moved by the twist of desperation of her painted lips, her too-eager friendliness. Her eyes were dark and afraid and her mouth quivered. He felt an immense sympathy for her. She was probably not a blatantly bad girl. Rather, she was a female mirror-image of himself, weak and confused. It struck him that neither of them had much of a chance to be anything better.

Opening his mouth to speak, Ralph discovered that his voice had deserted him. The girl was waiting, throwing nervous, fearful glances in the direction of the glowering saloonkeeper. Taking coins from his pocket, he put them on the bar. Her smile of thanks followed him as he made his way down the bar to where Chet Halleran was lifelessly flopping.

Standing a little way back, Richard Ralph spoke his brother-in-law's name commandingly.

'Chet.'

Raising his large, yellow-haired head from his arms, the unshaven Halleran looked angry and baffled. As he turned his head slightly and took in Richard Ralph, a thin edge of violence grew in his bloodshot eyes.

'Reader and Gaylor rode in without you this morning, Chet,' Ralph complained. 'Your sister's been worrying about you. She's in town now. Come on back to the ranch with us.'

Halleran made no reply, but the organ music died in a gurgle of notes. There was total silence, with the few people in the saloon immobile as if frozen. They feared for the insipid young man who had dared to address the foul-tempered young giant in that manner. The girth of one of Chet's muscular thighs was larger round than Richard Ralph's body. 'Big Maxie' Howland wore a pleased grin of anticipation as he watched the little drama being played out.

Halleran turned his head back facing the bar. Taking a step nearer to him, Ralph managed to say, 'Queenie wants you to . . .' before a back-handed swing of Halleran's massive left hand caught him full in the face.

Lifted completely off the ground by the force of the blow, Ralph sailed horizontally through the air, his body smashing explosively against a stack of crated bottles. To the accompaniment of the sound of breaking, tinkling glass, Richard Ralph's body crashed to the floor. He lay still. The girl with the wheat-coloured hair, concern on her face, started towards him, but a gruff, one-word order from the saloonkeeper stopped her in her tracks. The peg-leg knocked against the floor several times and the little man protested.

'This got to be stopped,' he said, but no one said a word or made a move.

But Ralph was stirring. His hands came up to grab the edge of a table. Slowly, so slowly that it was painful to watch, he pulled himself on to his feet in a hunched-over stance. With the back of his hand he wiped away the dark-red blood from where it leaked from his mouth and nose. All the movement did was to smear blood across his face as more poured from his split lips and damaged nose.

Though his legs wobbled, there was a kind of greatness to Richard Ralph as he made his way to where Halleran still sat with his arms resting on the bar. Swaying a little, struggling to regain his balance, Ralph stood behind his brother-in-law.

'Stop it, someone!' the blonde girl cried out. 'Chet will kill him.'

'This got to be stopped,' the peg-leg man repeated his earlier phrase.

'Keep out of this, Wobbler,' an unsympathetic Howland warned the man with the wooden leg. 'A man shouldn't pick a fight if he can't handle it.'

'That's true enough,' the musician agreed, absent-mindedly resting on his keyboard so that two notes blared out, startling everyone but Chet

Halleran, who appeared to have gone back to sleep.

Even the bloody-faced Richard Ralph looked round, staring bewildered at the organ until the sound had died away. Then he turned back to Halleran again, blood running from his face down on to his shirt. It was a ludicrous picture, the slight Ralph in an agitated state, keen to do battle with the massive, totally disinterested, Halleran.

'Turn around, Chet.'

Though Ralph's words were blurred by his mashed lips, what he had said was unmistakable. But Halleran ignored him. Ralph stood stiffly, teetering a little, gritting his teeth. Then he took everyone by surprise, possibly even himself, by smashing a right-handed punch into the side of Chet Halleran's face. For all Richard Ralph's lack of size and weight, the blow was a hefty one that visibly sent a tremor through Halleran's muscle-packed body.

A fresh cut on his cheek was visible as Halleran slowly turned to face his tormentor, seemingly unable to believe what had just taken place. But Ralph showed that he was in no doubt. Feinting with his left hand, he caused Halleran to automatically shift his head. This left him wide open to another right-hand punch that Ralph had already launched.

But with ridiculous ease, Halleran raised a thick arm to effortlessly deflect Ralph's blow. With the deliberate ease of someone doing some mundane task such as pouring a drink, Halleran cocked his right fist and drew it back. He started the fist for Ralph's face with all the power of his shoulder and twisting torso behind it. It landed with a sickening crunch, the knuckles shattering Ralph's face before the momentum of the punch sent his body flying through the air.

Ralph flew backwards to hit the wall. For what seemed an impossibly long time, Ralph defied gravity by seemingly adhering to the wall. Then he crashed to the floor in a heap. Those watching knew that this time he wouldn't get up.

Having remained seated throughout, Chet Halleran turned back to the bar and laid his yellow-haired head on his folded arms.

Three

All of Queenie's supplies had been loaded on the wagon. Worry had had her mind in too much of a turmoil to concentrate. Usually a fun day, the run into town had turned bitter. She knew that the fact that Richard was her husband would inflame Chet rather than pacify him. Though she was ashamed to accept it as the truth, there was a killer streak in her brother that frightened her terribly. Today it could peak; come to a head with the maiming or worse of her husband. Chilled by that possibility, she shuddered as she paid the storekeeper.

Outside, she was relieved to see that Marshal Graff was still keeping his daylight vigil close to the courthouse. If anything serious had taken place in the saloon, then Vern Graff would be attending to it. Except for the marshal the street was still deserted. At times like this some kind of sixth sense warned folk to keep themselves safe.

Then her heart skipped a beat as a man came at speed out through the doors of the Pleasure Palace. It wasn't Richard, but an undersized man who was

35

travelling so fast that he somersaulted off the sidewalk into the dirt of the street when he tried to
stop. It seemed that he had hurt his leg in the fall.
He scrambled upright and headed in her direction
with a limp that gave him an irregular, rolling gait.
Then she recognized "Wobbler" Turpin, the peg-
legged saloon roustabout.

Caked with dust from having taken a tumble, he
shouted her maiden name as he ran up. 'Queenie
Halleran, you'd better come quick!'

'Whatever is it?' she asked frantically as he
reached her, losing his footing and lurching against
the side of her wagon, grimacing in pain. Grabbing
him to prevent him from falling, Queenie held on to
Turpin while he massaged a hurt shoulder and
struggled to get his vocal cords working.

At last he gasped out his message. 'Your
brother's hurt Richard Ralph real bad.'

Head spinning, Queenie dreaded the reply to a
question she was compelled to ask. Maybe she was
the daughter of pioneers, but at that terrible
moment she wasn't the stuff her parents were
made of.

'Is Richard – dead?'

'Couldn't rightly say, Miss Halleran, but it's
awful bad.'

This was only half an answer, if it was any
answer at all. The softness left her, the hard world-
liness of a rancher's daughter surged into her eyes.
Her decision was an act of impulse. Lifting her
skirts, creating an indecent ankle-show but not
caring, she raced off down the street.

'Wait for me,' Wobbler Turpin yelled as he started a precarious run after her.

'What do they call you, stranger?' Vern Graff asked.

Roma shrugged. 'I guess that depends who's doing the calling, Marshal.'

'Right now it's Marshal Vern Graff who's asking your name.'

Straightening up in the saddle, Roma looked up and down the deserted street.

'In the circumstances, in a town that's about as lively as Boot Hill, Graff, I'd consider your question a mite unnecessary.'

'I decide what is and what isn't necessary in Minerva Wells. What handle do you go by?'

'Cado Roma,' Roma answered, taking his right foot out of the stirrup. Lifting the leg, he crooked it and rested it across the horn of his saddle.

'You're a hired gun, Roma, I can see that. You riding through?'

'No. Got myself work here.'

Graff's voice was icy as he sharply enquired, 'You been hired by the Slades?'

'That name means nothing to me, Marshal.' Roma brought his leg down and his foot found the stirrup. 'Right now, Graff, I'm going over to that saloon and buy myself a drink.'

'That isn't a good idea, Roma.'

'Seems to me it's the best idea I've had all day,' Roma disagreed.

'What if, Roma, I was to say that you should turn your bronc around and ride on out of town?'

'In that case I'd just ride on over to that saloon and buy myself that drink. Unless you can help me out by saying where I can find a man named Chet Halleran.'

The marshal's body tensed. He asked, 'What's your business with Chet Halleran?'

'Whatever it might be, it's my business, Graff,' Roma retorted.

'As from right now, Roma, I'm making it my business.'

Neither of them was prepared to back down, and an electrified tension was building between them. Then a woman came running wildly down the centre of the street, distracting them. Behind her, hopping and struggling to keep up, was a peg-legged man. The woman was making for the Pleasure Palace.

'Queenie!'

Queenie Ralph veered when Graff called her name. Roma saw her coming towards them. She darted a swift glance at Cado Roma. On recognizing him she looked startled. There was a note in her voice that was strange, registering her state of distress.

'Roma, what are you doing here?'

'You know this man, Queenie?'

'He's working for my father, Vern, supposedly keeping Chet on the straight and narrow.' Queenie was troubled, watching Graff intently. She frowned in perplexity, 'Wobbler says that Chet's hurt Richard real bad, Vern.'

'Well, I guess that's it, Queenie,' the marshal

said. 'I've got to go in there and bring Chet out. You go fetch Doc Ferris to have him see to Richard, Queenie.'

Nodding assent, Queenie ran off down the street, but as the marshal moved away towards the Pleasure Palace, Roma moved his horse to block the way.

'Best thing here, Graff, is for me to start earning the wage Halleran is paying me.'

'Tangle with Chet Halleran, Roma, and you could end up too dead to collect one single cent,' the marshal replied, trying to walk round Roma's horse. 'You could help out by keeping watch in case any of the Slade brothers come riding into town.'

Roma's horse blocked him again. 'I wouldn't know a Slade if I tripped over one.'

'You'd know them once you see them. They're real mean, Roma.'

'I'd hate to be mistaken about them,' Roma said with a shake of his head. 'You stay on the look-out for your Slades, Marshal, and I'll take care of Halleran.'

Though calm the marshal was alert, watching for signs that would help him to understand Roma. 'If I allow you to go in there, Roma, I want you to do it slow and easy.'

'I'll handle it,' Roma assured the marshal. 'I've played the game before, Graff.'

Riding at a slow gait, with the sun on his back, he reached the Pleasure Palace hitching rail. Dismounting as casually as a cowpuncher with nothing more serious on his mind than a first shot of red-eye, he patted the dust from his clothing with both hands.

Going inside, he took everything in with a single, sweeping glance. The heads of the few people present turned his way, except for the yellow-haired head of a giant of a man who was slumped on the bar, and the bloodily mashed head of Richard Ralph, who lay sprawled inertly on the floor in a corner. The lone bartender was polishing glasses like he was expecting a crowd of drinkers at any moment, and Roma judged the well-dressed bald man with red bushy sideburns who was watching him, to be the proprietor. A saloon girl with wheat-coloured hair knelt beside Ralph, using a bar towel in an attempt at stanching the bleeding from his mouth and nose. Entering the saloon behind Roma, the peg-legged man stumped noisily across to stand by the girl. The big man lying with his head on his arms had to be Chet Halleran. Roma was pacing slowly in his direction when the voice of the well-dressed man stopped him.

'Plenty of room to drink this end of the bar, stranger.'

'I prefer that end,' Roma answered as he moved on. He spoke loudly, 'Halleran.'

The yellow head stirred. The peg-legged man cautioned, 'Be mighty careful, stranger.'

Head coming up, Chet Halleran peered at Roma through bleary, bloodshot eyes, asking in a thick-tongued voice 'Do I know you?'

'I know you, and that's all that matters,' Roma answered. 'Move yourself, I'm taking you back to the Rainbow.'

Chuckling, Halleran gave a shrug of his massive shoulders, emphasizing the expanse of his barrel chest. His coarse, bloated face bore no resemblance whatsoever to that of his sister. Sliding off his stool, Halleran struck an aggressive pose, his thumbs stuck in his sagging gunbelt. There was a Navy Colt holstered at his right hip; a lighter calibre six-gun than Roma would have expected the huge man to favour.

'What name do you go by, stranger?'

'I'm Cado Roma.'

Halleran sneered. 'Never heard of you. So, you've come to take me back to the ranch?'

'That's why I'm here, Halleran.'

'Well now, I've a mind to stay here, but if you're intent on taking me back, you better start taking.'

As Roma moved closer to Halleran he heard the girl tending Ralph half-scream the word 'No!' It was a warning that Roma should have heeded. For all his bulk and drunken condition, Chet Halleran could move like lightning. A fist the size of a ham smashed into Roma's ribs to send him spinning back along the bar.

With all air driven out of his lungs by the blow, and new air refusing to be drawn in, everything was going dark for Roma. As his vision cleared he saw the girl, standing now looking his way, fear for him stamped like a mask on her face. A grinning Halleran was in the same position, fists cocked, waiting for him to try again, confidently inviting him to try again.

Shaking his head to clear it further, Roma moved slowly back down the length of the bar towards Halleran. Not having expected such speed from the big man, Roma had now learned his lesson. Roma had spotted the half-filled glass of whiskey that Richard Ralph had left on the bar. This time it was he who took Chet Halleran by surprise. Picking up the glass with his left hand, he tossed the contents straight into the huge man's eyes. Temporarily blinded, Halleran fumbled for the gun on his hip. But Roma's foot lashed out, the toe slamming into Halleran's groin. As his huge opponent doubled over, yelling out in agony, Roma drew his own gun and brought it swinging down in an arc. The barrel caught Halleran across the side of the head, instantly felling him.

But he was tough. Rolling on his side, using his left hand to wipe away the liquor that was stinging his eyes, he drew the Navy Colt with his right hand and fired. The bullet went wide of Roma, who stepped in to first kick the gun from Halleran's hand, then catch him a terrific kick to the jaw that had him slump back on the floor unconscious.

Suddenly aware of an incessant screaming coming from behind him, Roma spun round. The saloon girl was lying across a table, clutching at her left arm, screaming with pain as blood pumped from her shoulder. The peg-leg man was moving around in little agitated circles, wanting to do something to help the girl, but at a loss to know what.

*

The sound of a gunshot reached Queenie just as she and Doc Ferris came up to where Vern Graff was standing. The doctor, a tall, thin, gangling young man, hesitated when he heard the shot, placing the bag he was carrying on the ground.

'I'm not risking myself in there, Marshal,' Ferris said, 'until you find out what's happening.'

'Wait here, Queenie,' Graff ordered as he started at a run for the saloon.

Disobeying, Queenie was close on his heels. They looked in to see Chet Halleran prone on the floor, and Roma tending to a saloon girl who lay on a table, bleeding. Queenie gave a small groan when she saw her husband lying on the floor, his knuckle-mashed face as bloody as a slice of raw meat.

'Come on up, Doc, you're needed,' Vern Graff called over his shoulder as Queenie and himself hurried into the Pleasure Palace.

'What happened to the girl?' the marshal asked.

'Halleran done shooted her,' Wobbler Turpin complained. 'The poor gal didn't do nothing to deserve it. Ruth had been taking good care of Richard Ralph.'

'It wasn't Chet's fault, Graff. This stranger just kept prodding him and he was trying to defend himself,' the saloonkeeper volunteered.

'We'll get the rights and wrongs of it later, Howland,' Vern Graff said, as Doc Ferris entered the saloon and rushed to where the girl was stretched out on the table.

Taking a look at her wound, the doctor said to

Roma, 'You've done a good job there, stranger. I'll be back.' He dashed over to kneel by Queenie at the side of her stricken husband.

When Graff came to stand beside Roma, the girl opened her blue mascaraed eyes to look from one to the other of them, bemused.

'Am I bad hurt?'

'No,' Roma assured her. 'No bones broken. The bullet went straight through, Miss.'

A weak smile painted itself briefly on what must once have been a pretty face. 'It's a whole heap of time since anyone called me miss.'

'You haven't been mixing in the right company, Ruth.' The marshal smiled.

'Why did you brace Chet Halleran, stranger?' she asked, her brow laddering in a frown.

'I wish now that I hadn't. The bullet you stopped was meant for me,' Roma apologized.

'It's worth it to have the handsomest man ever in Minerva Wells treat me with respect.'

'It's a whole heap of time since anyone called me handsome.' Cado grinned at her.

'Now you're joshing me,' she complained, a sudden warmth reddening her cheeks.

'Now, young lady, let's take a look at you,' Doc Ferris said as he came up to them.

'How's Ralph, Doc?' the marshal asked.

'He'll have a sore face for quite a time, but he'll live,' Ferris answered. 'It could have been the end for him if this young lady hadn't kept his airways clear of blood.'

The girl looked embarrassed, and Roma asked:

'She's going to have to rest up for a spell, isn't she, Doc?'

'A week to ten days is my guess.'

'Have you got somewhere she can stay, Doc?'

'It's easy to tell you're a stranger in town,' the young doctor said as he dressed the wound in the girl's shoulder. 'All I've got is a room that's not big enough for me.'

'Then we'll have to put her up in a hotel room,' Roma declared. 'Is there a respectable hotel in town, Marshal?'

'There's only two, but the Cattlemen's is about the best.'

'Right I'll get her a room there.'

'Who's going to pay for that, Roma?' Vern Graff asked.

'Hal Halleran.'

The marshal looked dubious. 'I don't think Hal will take kindly to paying bed and board for a saloon girl.'

'His son is responsible, so I'll see that he does,' Roma declared.

Nodding, the marshal said, 'Be that as it may, Roma. I'm going to lock young Halleran up. The circuit judge is due in three weeks, and Chet can stand trial for shooting Ruth.'

'That will put me out of a job, Marshal,' Roma pointed out.

Walking over to pull a now half-conscious Halleran to his feet, Graff propped him against the bar, pulled his muscular arms behind his back and lashed his wrists together. As he pulled the rope

tight the marshal said, 'You can stay here in
Minerva Wells and earn your money, Roma. This
town's finances don't run to a deputy marshal. I'm
on my own, apart from Wobbler, who feeds any
prisoners and mops out the cells when necessary.'

'What are you suggesting, Graff?'

'The thing is, Roma, Chet will be in more danger
in jail than out here. He'll be a sitting target for the
Slade brothers. Hal Halleran will be ready to keep
on paying you.'

'The Halleran girl told me that her brother had
killed one of the Slades,' Roma said.

'Murdered Noah Slade is how I reckon it, Roma.
He shot the Slade boy in the back, but there are no
witnesses.'

'Letting the Slades finish him off wouldn't be a
bad thing,' Roma observed.

'I wouldn't argue with that, but my job is to
uphold the law.' Graff pulled a reeling Halleran
away from the bar.

'Hold on a minute.' Stopping the marshal from
taking Halleran away, Roma patted the big man's
clothes. He held up a thick roll of banknotes. 'This
will get a hotel room for the girl.'

'I didn't see you take anything.' Vern Graff's face
wore a mock-innocent expression.

Intent on helping Queenie get her husband up
on their wagon and started for home, and then
taking Ruth to a hotel, Roma was making his way
to where the injured man and girl were now seated
on round backed chairs. He was stopped by 'Big
Maxie' Howland. The saloonkeeper wore a

holstered gun partially hidden behind the skirts of his grey coat, and there was the strong bite of whiskey on his breath.

'We town folk like things to run along pretty much as they are, mister.'

'Are you making a point of some kind, Howland?' Roma impatiently enquired.

'What I'm saying, Roma, is that the Hallerans are held in high esteem around these parts,' Howland said in a sibilant hiss. 'I don't like what you did to young Chet, and I like it even less because you did it in my establishment. I don't want to see you in the Pleasure Palace again, and I'd prefer it if you left town.'

Roma walked to where the doctor had finished tending to Ralph and Ruth. He asked, 'What about the girl?'

'She's lost a lot of blood and, like I said, needs a week or two of rest.'

'I'll take care of the girl, Doc,' Howland gruffly interrupted.

Ignoring him, Roma looked across to where Ruth sat nursing her damaged shoulder. 'Do you think you're fit enough to walk? We'll fix you up with a comfortable room.'

'I'll give it a try,' the girl said gamely, allowing Roma to help her to her feet.

'Taking her out of here, Roma, will be your second big mistake today,' Howland said angrily. 'Your third mistake could well be your last.'

Four

It was the kind of night when the dark sky comes down and wraps itself around the world. Queenie strolled with Roma from the ranch house to where his horse stood waiting. Kalin, the spotted dog, walked faithfully at her heels. They had put Richard Ralph to bed. His face had swollen so badly that one of his eyes was completely closed and the other a mere slit that he must have had difficulty seeing through.

'You'll see that Chet comes to no harm won't you?' she asked Roma as he slowly untied the reins of his horse. Both of them were reluctant to part from each other.

Somewhere a little way off from where it was perched in a cottonwood tree, an owl added solemn and deep hoots to the mystery of the darkness. A sense of uneasiness disturbed Roma. Totally dependent on him in town were Chet Halleran and Ruth the saloon girl. Halleran didn't know that without Roma he was unlikely to stay alive for long, but it was different with Ruth.

48

Though frightened and insecure while working for Howland, she was terrified without the doubtful protection that came with her employment.

'I'm surprised you still have those kinds of feelings for your brother now, Queenie.'

'I'm not sure how I feel about him, Cado,' she said thoughtfully. 'I'm thinking of my parents. They both love him dearly, and dad has high hopes of Chet taking over the ranch one day.'

'Your brother is sure going to have to change a heap before that can happen.'

'I know,' she agreed pensively, lightly biting her bottom lip with even white teeth.

He was in the saddle, ready to leave. Queenie placed a hand on his leg. She said, 'I'm glad that you are here, Cado.' He sensed that she was blushing, but couldn't tell in the night. 'I shouldn't have said that.'

With no words coming to mind, Roma dug his heels into the flanks of his horse. As he rode off the darkness grew thicker and even the owl had stopped its hooting.

Standing inside the barred but unglazed window of his office, Vern Graff watched the Three Forks riders dismount outside the Pleasure Palace. Though he had seen no sign of the three Slade brothers, the marshal was sure that word of Chet Halleran's arrest had reached them. He had considered calling Wobbler Turpin in and arming him with a rifle. But all that would achieve would be to have the crippled man shot dead as well as Chet.

It was an immense relief for Graff to see Roma come riding slowly down the street. He looked lazy and contented in the way of a man about to pay a social call. But the marshal had known men like Roma before, and they never relaxed. The gunfighter passed the Pleasure Palace and rode slowly towards the Cattlemen's Hotel.

As a disappointed marshal watched the darkness swallow up Cado Roma, from the corner of his eye he saw four men furtively slip out through the door of the Pleasure Palace. All four moved quickly into the shadows. Something was afoot.

Reaching behind him for a rifle, Vern Graff checked the magazine. Whatever was happening out there on the street, he knew that he could expect trouble in a short while.

'Mister.'

Sitting up in bed, face white from loss blood, Ruth called his name as he was about to go out the door. The bedsheet was pulled up to her throat. Roma turned with a smile.

'Call me Cado.'

Her eyes were screwed up tight like she was thinking hard or was worried. Her features were modelled exquisitely. Her alive, blue eyes were framed in curves of brown eyebrows, and studded with long, moist lashes. She pointed to where he had propped his rifle in the corner of her room.

'You've forgotten your rifle.'

He explained, 'I'm only going over to the marshal's office, Ruth, I won't be long. I'll call in to see you on the way back, and collect it then.'

Though feeling refreshed after washing, he hadn't had a lot of rest since leaving Santa Fe. After checking to see if Vern Graff needed him, he would get some sleep.

'Cado.'

This time she called him by name as he was about to leave. She was staring at him strangely. He paused.

'Yes, Ruth?'

'Thank you for taking care of me.'

'I got you shot,' he humbly replied.

In the street at the side of the hotel the air was no longer musty with the dust driven up by the traffic of the day. There was a pale moon but the high buildings on each side made the street dark. He had walked only a short distance when his name was called from across the street.

'Roma.'

The man who called was no more than a blurred silhouette. There were three more men in addition to the one who had called to him. Along the street to his right, the misshapen shadow of what should have been an open doorway told him that a man was lurking there. Two men were outlined by the moon on the immediate horizon of the roofs of the buildings opposite.

'I've a message for you, Roma,' the man who had called said.

It had to be from Howland the saloonkeeper, Roma reasoned. Having earlier told him to get out of town, Howland had sent four guns to make sure that he either left or he died.

He asked, 'What message?'

'It comes from the Slade boys,' the man across the street answered, causing Roma to think again. 'They don't want you messing with the business they have with Chet Halleran. This ain't no concern of your'n, Roma. You leave the marshal to do his job and we'll make sure that you ride safely out of town.'

'I don't plan on leaving,' Roma said. 'Right now I'm going over to the jail.'

'You got that wrong, mister. We've been sent to see that you don't go nowhere near the marshal's place.'

Aware of the four men getting ready for action, Roma cursed his stupidity in leaving his rifle in the hotel. Though confident that he could get the man across the street with his six-gun, the distance between him and the other three men made a rifle essential. He was wracking his brain for a plan that might improve his chances, when he was forced to make a move on hearing from across the street the smallest of metallic *clicks* that could have been made by a rifle bolt. That was all, but Roma could take no risks in his situation.

Drawing his gun, Roma fired from the hip then dropped to the boardwalk. The dull thud of a falling body signalled that he had scored a hit across the street. But then three rifles opened fire. Bullets slammed into the hotel wall above and on each side of him and splinters of wood flew dangerously close to his face. Roma could do noth-

ing but lie flat on the sidewalk close in to the wall.
The chances of hitting any of those gunning for
him were remote, and the flash of his revolver
would give them his exact position. The firing
ceased, but the night held the rolling thunder of it
for some time. A deep silence followed. Then he
caught a slight sound from across the street. First
it was a bubbling cough. This was following by a
gushing sound that he identified. It was blood
squirting out under great pressure. His slug must
have caught the man across the street in the
neck, severing all connections with the head.
Roma had known this before. For a while the
heart doesn't know that its vital centre has been
cut off and for a while it goes on pumping blood.

'Is he hit?'

This cautious enquiry was called from a rooftop
down to the man in the doorway along the street.
Roma knew that the question asked was about him.

'Reckon so, pard, but I can't rightly tell.'

'Go take a look, Ed,' the second man up high on
the buildings suggested more than ordered.

'Take a look yourself,' Ed, the man in the street
retorted. 'I heard about this Cado Roma when I
was down in New Mexico. He ain't the sort of
hombre you walk up on.'

They were novices. Though in no doubt of this,
Roma didn't underestimate the enemy. He was
outnumbered and they had rifles while he didn't.
He heard more advice called down in a shaky-
sounding voice.

'Then don't walk up on him, just keep yourself

hid and go take a look,' came the advice from on high.

Lying flat, Roma put his ear to the wooden sidewalk. It acted as a sounding-board and he could hear the slow plod of footsteps. They were becoming gradually louder, but Roma realized that it was impossible to judge how far away the man was. Gripping his .45, he waited. When the man got close enough Roma would have no option but to chance a shot. That might save him from the rifle of the man on the street, but would expose him as a target to the two riflemen up on the roof. All he could do was wait. He estimated that he had three miutes at the most.

When the sound of gunfire rent the night air, Vern Graff scanned the darkness of the town through the window of his office. Then he saw the flashes: blends of yellow, red and blue as rifles were fired from the rooftops next to the hotel. His practised eye picked out the flare from another rifle. It was down on the street. Making calculations fast, running the possibilities through his mind, he concluded that men from Three Forks had ambushed Cado Roma. The Slade brothers must have learned, probably from Max Howland, that Roma would be sharing the guarding of Halleran with him. They wanted nothing of Roma except that he be dead, so that when their men drew him out of his office to deal with trouble in the saloon, Chet Halleran would be alone, trapped in a cell.

The Slades were nerveless, brooding men. For

them the quick kill was not the perfect answer for revenge. They were men who would enjoy the waiting. Chet Halleran would be made to suffer horrifically. Obadiah, Shem, and Eli Slade would wallow in the contemplation of their victim's death. They would savour Halleran's anguish like a fine whiskey.

Marshal Graff needed to reach a decision in a hurry. The Three Forks ranch had no gunfighters on its payroll; just ordinary cowhands knocked into line by their ruthless bosses. If it wasn't too late, he could make it across to the hotel. Roma and himself would make a duo against which the Three Forks' cowpokes wouldn't stand a chance. They wouldn't know how to handle the fight when it came back on them and exploded in their faces. Obviously, the Slade brothers didn't intend to ride into town until later. Graff's dilemma came from the possibility that Roma had already been downed, and if he was to go to find out, there might be more Three Forks hands waiting to take over the jail and wait for their bosses to arrive.

Frustrated, wondering what the absence of further gunfire meant, Marshal Graff decided that his priority lay in guarding the jail. Though he had no liking for any of the three Slade brothers, he recognized that they had a genuine grievance. But even though he shared their knowledge that brother Noah had been shot in the back by Halleran, and that there were witnesses to the killing who wouldn't come forward, it was his duty to uphold the law.

Suddenly, with a renewed burst of gunfire coming from the direction of the hotel, Graff's logic and resolve was demolished. Cado Roma must still be alive, but not for much longer.

The man stalking him was close now. Roma silently eased himself up into a kneeling position. To stay lying flat, or to make a sound, would be suicidal in this situation. There was an alcove in the wall at his back. Formed when an extension of some kind had been added to the hotel, it was narrow, but when he was on his feet he discovered that he could squeeze into it.

With the sound of the tiptoeing man growing louder, Roma concealed himself as much as possible in the alcove. Carefully holstering his gun, he drew a long-bladed knife from his belt, and waited.

Rifle held at waist level, the man was slowly approaching. His steps had become hesitant as he neared to find no sign of Roma. The man stopped. With his back pressed hard against wall, Roma silently urged him to come on. He did, taking one very slow and cautious step at a time. Aware that the two men on the rooftops were awaiting developments, ready to fire if and when a target was revealed to them, Roma fought impatience until the man drew level with him.

Snaking out his left arm, Roma wrapped it tight round the man's neck, fingers gripping his throat. He was young, his body hardly fully formed. He was also very frightened. In the dull glow of moonlight, his eyes were funny as they looked at Roma. They had an oblique quality as if they were looking into the next world while still in this one. They watched and waited.

Roma swiftly brought the knife up, aiming for the soft centre just below the breastbone. But something, probably the instinct of self preservation, made the young cowboy he was holding try to defend himself by bringing his rifle up. The blade of Roma's knife came hard against the stock of the weapon, deflecting the blade. The blade was diverted. Instead of making a fast, smooth entry it hit the man's rib cage. Feeling his knife skidding off bone, Roma reacted. Twisting the hand holding the knife so that the blade went through a quarter turn, he drove it hard in between the cowpuncher's ribs.

It was a fatal wound, but not the quick, silent kill that Roma had planned. Withdrawing the knife, he released the man, who flopped down on to the sidewalk. Roma was relieved that the cowboy's collapse was a sagging, flopping movement that wouldn't have been heard by the two men on the rooftops.

But then his luck ran out completely. The mortally wounded man lying at his feet started to scream. At first his scream was like that of a woman, so high-pitched as to be almost noiseless. But then, in his frenzy of pain, his cry became a whistle-like screaming that tore the night apart.

The horrific sound ended abruptly when the rifles opened up from on high across the street.

The first bullet thudded into the sidewalk; the second slammed into the body of the cowboy, cutting him off in mid-scream. With nowhere to hide, Roma pressed himself tight against the wall as the fusillade of ripping, tearing, wood splintering bullets appeared to be seeking him in the dark. It could only be a matter of minutes before a bullet found him. He considered running, but to do so was likely to hasten his end.

'Cado.'

A woman's voice called from above. Tipping his head back, he looked up to see the head and shoulders of Ruth leaning out of the window of her room. Fear for her had him about to shout a warning, to tell her to go back in, when he saw her drop his rifle. The weapon came plummeting down towards him. Raising his right hand, he caught the rifle. As he did so, Roma did a forwards dive off the sidewalk to roll head over heels in the dust of the street.

With all his finely tuned reflexes working in unison, he came into a half-sitting, half-lying posture and he brought his rifle up into a firing position. With bullets still tearing slivers of wood from the sidewalk behind him, Roma concentrated on the rifle flashes flaring on the roof to his right. Pulling the trigger, he didn't wait to check the result. He was confident that he had hit the man. A bullet ploughed across the back of his left hand as he aimed at the second man. The slug left a burning track along the flesh, but this didn't affect either Roma's aim or his capability. He fired, seeing a shadow that suggested that the man was falling from the roof, and then a thudding crash on the sidewalk confirmed that this was so.

Out of danger now, he got to his feet. He hurried to the far side of the street and moved into the shadows, watching and waiting to be sure that the sound of gunfire hadn't brought others to back up the men he had shot. Roma glanced up at Ruth's window. It was closed and she was nowhere to be seen. An oil-lamp still burned inside the room. To Roma, it was a warm glow that was somehow symbolic of the courageous and inventive girl. He had been in her debt before, now he owed her everything. He owed her his life.

There was what could be a movement in the shadows further along the street. About 300 feet away, it could have been a trick of light, a vagrant breeze, or even the scampering of a small animal. But Roma took no chances. Bringing his rifle to bear in that direction he called in a low voice, 'Whoever you are, come out into the street, real slow. Move, or I'll blast you.'

'Hold it, Roma. It's me, Marshal Graff.'

Relieved, Roma walked forward. 'You should know it's dangerous to lurk in the shadows, Vern.'

They met where the man who had fallen from the roof lay huddled. A dark, misshapen mass folded into the ground the way a dead body does. Looking down at the body, Graff commented, 'Seems like it's a damned sight safer in the shadows, Roma.'

'There were four of them,' Roma reported, not mentioning Ruth's contribution to the fight. Taking off his bandanna, he wrapped it round his left hand. Blood, warm and sticky, had run down to collect between his fingers.

'There's no need me asking if you got them all.' That was the only comment that the marshal made. Men such as Cado Roma had their own vanity in this business of killing, and to question them could be construed as a criticism of their skill.

'They claimed to be Slade men.'

'They claimed rightly,' the marshal nodded. 'I've got to make it back to the jail, Cado, or else there'll be no Chet Halleran to go back to. You coming along?'

Alerted by the sound of gunfire, men and women were spilling out of the Pleasure Palace into the dark street. They were curious as to what had been happening, but Roma and the marshal pushed through them wordlessly.

'I'll check out the jail with you,' Roma assented, 'then I've got to get me some shut eye.'

Urgency in his stride, the marshal said, 'That's fine by me. It will help if you could give me a few hours' break in the morning.'

'I'll be there,' Roma promised, then swiftly added a warning. 'There's three riders coming.'

'I know.'

Although, strictly speaking, they were on different sides of the fence, events were uniting Roma and Graff. They stood side by side in the middle of

the street just short of the jailhouse. Holding their
rifles with a deceptive looseness, they waited for
the three slow-moving riders to reach them. The
trio reined up. One was a gaunt, hollow-eyed man
with a heavy black moustache. The second was
slim with almost delicate facial features and a
complexion that was almost transparent. Though
he had a sickly look about him in a country of
sunburned men, there was an indefinable something about this second rider that said he had
hidden strengths, hidden ability as a fighting
man. Perhaps ten years younger than the other
two, the third man ran to fat, but that didn't
disguise the bulging muscles that lay beneath a
layer of surplus flesh.

'This is Obadiah, Shem and Eli Slade,' Graff
informed Roma, indicating the riders left to right
as they reined up. The trio had ridden into town
from the south so that the open range and the
moon wouldn't be behind them. Then the marshal
spoke to the elder brother, the one with the moustache.

'There's four of your men lying dead at the side
of the Cattlemen's Hotel, Obadiah.'

All three of the brothers stared stonily at the
marshal. All three were hostile. It was the
youngest, the heavily-built Eli, who eventually
spoke. His eyes were without colour. They seemed
to look right through a man. His voice was quiet,
rather subdued, but it held a thin truculence.

'You should know better than to go killing
Three Forks men, Marshal.'

'Marshall Graff didn't kill them. I did,' Roma volunteered.

In unison, the three heads of the riders moved slowly in his direction. Three pairs of eyes stared coldly at Roma. At his side, Vern Graff's hands tightened on his rifle. The atmosphere was icy.

Five

Tall in the saddle, Obadiah Slade made a forbidding figure in the half-light. He wore a dark-grey suit, white shirt with a stand-up collar, and a black string tie. His gaunt face and hollow eyes gave him the impoverished appearance of a travelling preacher, but that was where any resemblance to a man of the cloth ended. There was an air of ruthlessness and menace about him as he stared down at Roma, but he addressed Vern Graff in a voice that was a grating half-whisper. 'You got yourself a deputy, Marshal?'

'No, I'm still the only law in Minerva Wells,' Graff replied.

Turning his head very slowly to fix the gaze of his deepset eyes on the marshal, Obadiah then brought his cold stare back to Roma. He asked in a way that demanded an answer, 'Then who might you be, stranger?'

Holding Obadiah Slade's gaze, Roma took a tobacco sack from his pocket. Unhurried, he rolled himself a cigarette. Licking the paper and sealing it before replying, he then said, 'Cado Roma.'

'That's a name that means nothing to us,' Shem Slade put in. He had a soft, conversational way of speaking that was in keeping with his sickly looks.

'Which raises a mighty big question,' Obadiah frowned.

'Which is,' Shem said, 'why would a stranger kill Three Forks men?'

'Exactly,' the hoarse-voiced Obadiah backed up his brother.

'They dry-gulched me,' Roma said, striking a match and lighting his cigarette.

'Where did this happen?' Shem Slade enquired, friendly like.

'Like Marshal Graff told you,' Roma replied tiredly, 'alongside the Cattlemen's Hotel.'

Shem Slade gave an indifferent shrug. 'We've only got your word for that.'

'Exactly.' Obadiah nodded. 'Now why would our boys bother to jump a stranger?'

'Maybe you brothers know the answer to that, Obadiah,' Vern Graff said sharply.

'You were there, Marshal,' Obadiah asked mildly, mockingly.

'You should have said, Vern.' Shem carried on his brother's charade.

'I wasn't there but . . .'

'There are no *buts* if you weren't there, Vern,' Shem advised.

'Exactly,' Obadiah agreed. 'So, you'll be taking this Roma in for shooting our men, Marshal.'

'I heard enough at the time, and saw enough afterwards, Obadiah,' Vern Graff said evenly, 'to be satisfied that it happened the way Roma said.'

'But we aren't satisfied. We aren't satisfied with the way the law is upheld in this town.'

'That's your privilege, Obadiah,' Graff said quietly. 'But I'm the only law that Minerva Wells has got, so there isn't much you can do about that.'

'We can make our own law,' Obadiah argued.

'I wouldn't advise that,' the marshal cautioned.

'It's simple enough.' Shem gave Graff a friendly smile. 'Right now we can make a start by having brother Eli teach Roma here a lesson that he won't forget in a rush.'

Eli Slade was swinging one leg over his saddle to dismount while this conversation was going on. But Vern Graff had raised his rifle to cover Obadiah Slade. He hissed a warning.

'Tell Eli to stay on his horse. Move as much as an eyelid, Obadiah, and I'll blow you out of the saddle.'

'You can't get all three of us, Marshal.'

'You'll already be dead, Obadiah, so that won't matter to you,' Vern Graff pointed out.

Eli was in the act of dismounting, with one foot still in the stirrup. Stooping to lay his rifle down, Roma took a step forward to grab the heavily built Slade brother's free foot. Heaving upward, Roma spun Eli in a cartwheel. The horse panicked, squealing as it rose up on its rear legs, then raced off down the street. With one foot caught in a stir-

rup, Eli Slade was dragged along, his head and
shoulders bouncing on the ground.

Eli made howling, pitiful cries like those of a
wounded animal. Obadiah Slade reined his horse
about and drove in the spurs to go galloping off in
pursuit of the bolting horse. Apparently unmoved
by what was going on, Shem Slade gave a soft
laugh as if what was happening to his youngest
brother was a joke, but he was staring at Roma.
Then he wheeled his horse around and rode off at
a walking pace, heading for where Obadiah had
stopped the runaway horse. The screams of Eli
Slade had become a whimpering that reached to
where Graff and Roma stood in the street. The
three Slades rode out of town with Obadiah holding the reins of Eli's horse, leading it. The massive
figure of the youngest Slade was slumped over,
head down.

'They'll be back, Cado,' Vern Graff warned.

'I had it figured that way, Vern,' Cado nodded.
'I'll go with you to check on Halleran, then I'll get
me some shut-eye and come on back over to the
jail so's you can take a break.'

'We need to take as good care of Ruth as we do
of Chet Halleran, for different reasons,' Graff
said. 'I'll need her to give evidence against
Halleran when the judge gets here.'

Roma nodded. 'I know that, Vern. Don't worry,
I've got more reason to look after her.'

'This town hasn't given you much of a welcome,
Cado.'

Shrugging, Roma said, 'I've known worse.'

'I guess,' the marshal commented with a small, tight grin.

Waking up suddenly, Queenie Ralph listened fearfully for her husband's breathing. With relief, she heard the regular rhythmic breaths of the sleeping Richard. Her husband had taken a terrible beating, and, already weakened by illness, he would have succumbed in the night. Richard had an inner core of strength that was a great credit to him.

It was early. Five o'clock, the unsmiling hour when the light showed the rugged terrain in all its harshness through the ranch house window. She noticed that the wind had changed, from a north-east round to a south-west, the rainbringer. The sun was anxious to be seen, parting heavy curtains of cloud, but as Queenie looked further out into the distance, darkness came chasing over the hills.

Trouble was gathering around the Hallerans as surely as rainclouds were darkening the horizon. Queenie rested for a moment before trying to work out what to do in the immediate future. She couldn't conceal Chet's behaviour from her mother – Richard was too broken and bruised for that. He stirred as she got out of bed, peering at her through the slit of one slightly less damaged eye.

'Lie still,' she told him as she dressed herself. 'I'll make you some breakfast.'

'No.' The one-word objection was blurred as it

passed through swollen lips that had split when punched against his teeth. But Richard was determined. Propped up on both elbows, he said, 'I'm not staying in bed. Help me out when you are ready, Queen.'

'You must stay there, Richard. You have to rest.'

'No,' he protested, forcing the issue by scrambling to the side of the bed so that she had to rush to his side and assist him. 'No more, Queen. I've been pushed around enough, and I'll have no more of it. From this moment onwards, Richard Ralph is fighting back.'

There was a kind of grandeur to him that made Queenie feel terribly disloyal. She was anxious to go into Minerva Wells to discover what was happening there. She felt all the guiltier because she knew that Cado Roma would be in town.

His slurred words were easy to interpret. 'You are the one that I have to prove myself to.'

Saddened, she was close to tears when helping him to dress. The massive bruising of his body appalled her. She went down the stairs ahead of Richard, with him resting a hand on each of her shoulders for support. Kalin, the dog, greeted them excitedly. After helping her husband into a chair, Queenie was making coffee and frying bacon when her mother came down.

Muriel Halleran recoiled at the sight of her son-in-law. She gasped, 'My word, Richard! What on earth happened to you?'

'A horse threw . . .' Richard attempted a lame excuse, but Queenie interrupted him. Her mother wasn't easily fooled. Queenie accepted that she had no alternative but to tell the truth. Even so, she wanted to tell the story in easy stages.

'Sit down, Mother, and I'll explain after you have some coffee.'

But the older woman didn't sit. She refused to do so. Taking a few steps closer to Richard, she peered at him before turning to Queenie and saying in a strained voice, 'Chet did this, didn't he?'

Busying herself at the stove, Queenie delayed giving the answer. Her mother slumped into a chair, elbows on the table, holding her head in her hands. A silent sobbing was shaking her body, showing that she knew the truth before Queenie said another word.

'Yes, it was Chet,' Queenie confirmed.

Muriel Halleran asked, 'Where is Chet now?'

'There's more to it than what he did to Richard, Mother.'

'Oh, God! How bad is it? What has he done now, Queenie?'

'Leave it for now, Mother,' Richard mumbled. 'I'm sure that it will all work out.'

'What will work out, Richard? I need to know, Queenie.'

Queenie took a deep breath. 'Chet didn't only hurt Richard, mother.'

'What else did he do? I have to know, Queenie.'

'I realize that, mother,' Queenie replied. 'It's just that I wish that I didn't have to be the one to tell, Chet shot a saloon girl.'

'He killed her?' Muriel Halleran's face was ashen.

'No.' Queenie shook her head. 'But she's hurt bad.'

'Where's Chet now?'

'Vern Graff's got him in the jail. I imagine that he'll hold him for the circuit judge.'

Hands covering her face, Muriel Halleran moaned, 'We have to get your father back.'

'We can't do that!' Queenie was shocked. Apart from his family, the cattle drive to the railhead was the most important thing in Hal Halleran's life.

'We have to Queenie,' Muriel Halleran insisted. 'Your father must be here.'

'Dad hired the new man, Cado Roma, to take care of Chet.'

'That man hasn't done very well so far,' Muriel Halleran said with a scornful snort.

'That's not fair, he . . .' Queenie began until she realized how stoutly she was defending Roma; she blushed red as she stopped herself from saying more. She covered her embarrassment by putting a bowl of food on the floor for Kalin. The dog hungrily wolfed the meat down.

'But he'll do,' the mother said. 'We must send this Roma man after your father.'

'That's not possible, mother.'

'Why ever not?'

'If Marshal Graff doesn't have Roma help him guard the jail, then the Slade brothers will kill Chet,' Queenie explained.

The truth of this slowly dawned on her mother. 'I see. Oh dear, what a terrible situation we are in, Queenie. Whatever will we do?'

'There's no way we can get word to Father,' Queenie said adamantly. 'Danny Reader is out riding line, so we only have Jack Gaylor here at the ranch, and we can't manage without him.'

'That's true. We can't spare either of them,' a desperate Muriel Halleran agreed. 'One man can't take care of everything here.'

With a struggle, Richard Ralph got to his feet. Bent over, clinging to the table with both hands to keep himself from falling, he had beads of sweat appearing on his brow as he swayed.

'Sit down, Richard, please,' Queenie pleaded. 'You look terrible.'

Remaining standing, with difficulty, Richard said in a weak voice, 'I'll ride out to fetch Hal back.'

'You can't go,' Queenie protested, concern raising her voice to a shout.

'Trust me, Queenie,' he said, his voice growing stronger and resolve seeming to replace his physical weakness with something closely resembling strength.

'We won't let you go, Richard,' Muriel Halleran told him firmly. 'It's out of the question.'

'I'm going, Queenie, Mother. If I have to ride as far as Kansas City I will. I swear to you that I'll catch up with Hal and bring him back.'

'Tell him that he can't go, Mother,' Queenie begged, aware that she had no chance of persuading Richard, who could be infuriatingly obdurate.

'Pack me some jerky, some beans and some coffee, Mother,' Richard ordered with a self assurance neither Queenie nor her mother had witnessed in him before. Facing Queenie, he said, 'Get my gun and gunbelt from the drawer, please.'

Queenie's mouth opened, but no words came out. Fear for him had made her speechless.

Then she managed to say, 'But, Richard, you are no gunman, and you're certainly not fit for a long ride after the herd.'

'Don't underestimate me, Queenie,' he said sharply, hurt in his eyes.

'I am not,' she protested, knowing that she was lying, not believing for a moment that he could make the long ride through dangerous territory.

'I'm capable of using a gun, Queenie, and I am stronger than you think,' he argued, not angrily but almost pleading with his wife to give him some credence.

There was a dragging period of silence in which all three of them stood as unmoving as statues. It was Muriel Halleran who broke that awkward interlude by accepting that her son-in-law wouldn't be deterred. She moved towards a cupboard.

'I'll pack what you will need, Richard,' she said quietly.

'I guess that's the best plan,' an uncertain Vern Graff muttered.

'It's the *only* way,' Cado Roma insisted. 'The two of us can't protect Halleran from the Slades for three weeks, Vern.'

It was coming up to noon as they sat in the marshal's office drinking coffee. After giving Ruth breakfast and checking that she would be comfortable and safe while he was gone, Roma had come to the jail and given Graff a few hours' break. They had arranged that at noon the marshal would go across to the hotel for a meal, and Roma would go when he came back. But now they were discussing the scheme that Roma had suggested.

He proposed that, under cover of darkness, Roma, with Wobbler Turpin, would sneak Chet Halleran out of town. With supplies loaded on a packhorse, they would take the prisoner out to the distant Rainbow line shack where Roma had met Reader and Gaylor while looking for Chet. Halleran would be left there with Turpin guarding him, and be brought back to town in time to appear before the judge.

Graff didn't know the shack, and he questioned Roma anxiously.

'It's a long chance, I know that, but what if the Slade brothers should find out where we're holding Halleran? Wobbler wouldn't have a chance.'

'That's not so,' Roma argued. 'There's no way they could ride up to the shack without Wobbler knowing, and there's a ridge at the back of the place from which one man with a rifle could hold off the Seventh Cavalry.'

A worried frown wrinkled the marshal's brow. 'Wobbler's a handyman, not a hard man, Cado. I'd be worried leaving him out there alone with

Halleran. Chet's real smart, Cado. He's capable of fooling Wobbler, and wouldn't think twice about killing him.'

'I'll chain Halleran up so's Wobbler won't have any problem,' Roma assured Graff. 'Chet suffering for three weeks won't worry me.'

'Me neither, I'd put a bullet into his useless head if it weren't against the law, Cado. It's Wobbler I care about.'

A back-up idea came suddenly to Roma. 'Young Danny Reader is riding line on the Rainbow, Vern. I'll pick him up on the way to the shack. He can stand guard over Halleran with Wobbler.'

'Fine,' the marshal agreed. 'That makes me feel a lot easier.'

'Good. Now, you go and get yourself fed,' Roma said.

When Graff had left the office, Halleran shouted from the cage at the rear of the building.

'Hey, you out there! I heard your name, but, dang me, I've plumb gone and forgotten it.'

Getting up from his seat, Roma walked down a passageway and stood looking at Halleran through the bars.

'My name's Cado Roma.'

'Well, Roma,' Halleran moved forwards to grip the bars with both of his huge hands, 'you ain't got no business in Minerva Wells. How come you dealt yourself a hand in this little game?'

Contempt in his eyes, Roma looked steadily at the prisoner before saying sneeringly, 'A little game? Is that what you call roughing up a man less than half your size, and shooting a young girl?'

'I didn't ask you to judge me, Roma. I wanna know how you came to be mixed in this.'

'Your father hired me.'

Dismissing this with a violent shaking of his head, Halleran said, 'That ain't the case, Roma. If the old man did hire you, then you'd be riding drag to the railhead right now.'

'Halleran didn't hire me for the trail drive. He took me on to look after a son who's built like a man but acts like a baby.'

Knuckles whitening as he tightened his grip on the bars, Halleran's face went crimson with rage.

'You got a mouth that will cause you a lot of trouble, Roma.'

'Telling the truth never caused me no trouble, Halleran.'

Hunching his wide shoulders, Chet Halleran muttered, 'Why would the old man want you to look out for me, Roma? I could take you on one-handed while I'm eating my dinner.'

Roma grinned at him. 'That's just why Hal Halleran did hire me, because I've spent most of my life putting a bullet between the eyes of bragging fools like you, Halleran.'

Silent for a few moments, Chet Halleran then sneered; 'If the old man's paying you to take care of me, then you ain't earned your money. You'd better get the key and let me out of here, or the old man will feed you to the first hungry lion down from the mountains next winter.'

'I won't be letting you out, Halleran.'

'Come on, Roma. Unlock this danged door and you and me can settle what's between us here and now. Guns, knives or fists. The choice is yours.'

'My choice is to leave you there.'

'I guess you ain't got the craw to do otherwise,' Halleran said derisively.

'Marshal Vern will be holding you for the judge,' Roma said, turning away.

'That'll be old Judge Cronin,' Halleran chuckled. He then raised his voice as Roma was walking away. 'Let me tell you something, Roma. My old man's owned Cain Cronin this past twenty years. I won't get nothing but a friendly pat on the head.'

Roma came back to stand close to the bars. His voice was icy as he made a promise.

'In that case, Halleran, take my word for it. I will kill you before I leave Minerva Wells.'

Before moving away, Roma was rewarded by seeing fear in Halleran's eyes as the big man cowered from him.

Six

Late in the afternoon, Queenie Ralph glanced worriedly through a grey drizzling rain at the marshal's office as she reined up at the hitching rail. Though she had no way of seeing inside, there was a sense of emptiness to the place. Dismounting, she was relieved to see Vern Graff open the door and step out. Queenie quickly studied his face, ready to read any trouble that might show on it. But Vern Graff greeted her with a grin that twisted up one corner of his wide mouth. Already frantically concerned for Richard, who had ridden out hours ago, grimacing with pain at every movement of his horse, Queenie didn't want any additional worry. Looking quickly around her, eager for a glimpse of the handsome Cado Roma, she was both disappointed at not seeing him, and angry with herself for what was a betrayal of her husband.

'Afternoon, Queenie,' Graff said, giving his Stetson a little gentlemanly lift. 'If you've ridden in to see your brother, then I'm afraid that you're out of luck.'

'Why, what's happened, Vern?'

Her whole body was suddenly icy cold with dread, but she was quickly reassured.

'I'm right sorry, Queenie,' Graff said. 'I didn't intend to alarm you. Cado Roma and me thought it best for Chet's own safety to keep him out of town until Judge Cronin gets here.'

'Where is he?'

'Begging your pardon, Queenie, but it's probably better that you don't know that. So far as anyone else is concerned, Chet is still locked up.'

If the Slade brothers learned Chet had been moved out then they were likely to kill the marshal for duping them. But that possibility didn't worry the brave Vern Graff. Queenie had always admired him and men like him. Men like Cado Roma.

'You're expecting trouble, aren't you, Vern?' Queenie said in a hushed voice.

'Chet and trouble go together, Queenie.'

'You don't have to tell me that,' she commented with a weak smile. Then she went on to tell Graff a white lie. 'I've really come into town to see the girl who got hurt.'

'Ruth?' Vern Graff's face registered his surprise. 'She's not your sort, Queenie.'

'Maybe not, but I owe the girl a visit. It was my brother who shot her, Vern.'

Giving her a fond look, the marshal said, 'I guess that's the way you are, Queenie.'

'Like you said, Vern, it's the way I am.' Queenie smiled as she walked away.

When Queenie got over to the hotel, Maggie

Rumbold, the proprietor, showed a surprise similar to that of the marshal. But Maggie made no comment when showing Queenie up to a room in which she found a flaxen-haired girl propped into a sitting position in bed. Queenie found herself facing a sweet, shy, person who greeted her warmly and politely.

Pale from a loss of blood, Ruth's face could only manage a light pink in embarrassment as Queenie took an assortment of fruit from a bag and placed it on a small table.

'That's very kind of you, but you shouldn't have, Mrs Ralph,' the saloon girl protested.

'Queenie,' Queenie corrected her. 'You are a good, kind girl who tended to my husband.'

That exchange between them was initially stiff and awkward, but the situation eased when Queenie sat on the bed and they began to chat to each other comfortably. Ruth told her that she intended to leave Minerva Wells once she was fit enough to do so. She spoke of her determination to break away from working in a saloon. Queenie discovered that Ruth had no definite plans for the future, but a real determination to start afresh.

Queenie enjoyed talking to the girl so much that she didn't want to leave. She hadn't realized how much she had missed in life by not having the company of a girl of her own age. But she gave Ruth's hand an affectionate squeeze as she stood up from the bed to leave.

A frowning, blushing Ruth broke an awkward silence with a question.

'Did you happen to see Cado Roma anywhere?'

'No. Marshal Graff told me that he would be out of town for a while.'

'Oh.' Ruth's obvious disappointment was matched by the jealousy that Queenie felt, and was bitterly ashamed of.

Shortly before sundown on his second day out from the Rainbow ranch, Richard Ralph was in a rugged sweep of towering rocks and sand-hills when he saw a spiral of black smoke against the sky up ahead. There was every chance that bandits waited in ambush among the tangled rocks he must pass through. His immediate thought was to make a diversion, but he cancelled that out. Having at first been slowed down by a driving rain, he had since made good time. Ralph made a firm decision. No one, whoever it might be, and no matter how many of them there were, was going to deter him from his mission. There was a growing resentment in him. He had become a whipping-boy. Things couldn't go on as they were with Chet, or at the ranch, or in Minerva Wells.

As a precaution, he levered a shell into his rifle. The ride hadn't cured the agony of his battered body, but it had kind of numbed it. The hurt was still there, but it distressed him in a different, easier way. He swung into a narrow defile. From a tangle of greasewood, he looked down into a canyon where a tiny wisp of smoke hung ghostlike a few feet above the ground in the centre of a large clearing. The area was deserted, but whoever had been there had left just a short while ago.

He dismounted in the clearing and walked to where a small fire had recently been burning, and a coffee-pot had been overturned on the steaming rocks. Someone, perhaps aware of his approach, had left here hurriedly.

A mile further on, with lengthening shadows warning that night was close, Ralph sensed that he was being watched. The eerie experience was a sensation like an icy finger being run down his spine. Whoever had been at the camp-fire had concealed himself or themselves somewhere on the slopes until after he had passed. What could they want with him? That was a pointless question. Out here there were men desperate enough to kill for the rifle he carried, or even for the pack of dried meat in his saddle-bag.

There was a full moon by the time he had found suitable camping place. Though he had seen nothing of his pursuers, he had studied the terrain with care. Eventually he chose a hilltop ringed by boulders and brush. No one could approach without being seen, Although that provided a sense of security, Ralph had to face the reality of not being able to keep watch. It would mean putting himself at risk, but he desperately needed sleep.

Not risking a fire that would be seen for miles up here on the hill, he took out some jerky and chewed on it steadily. A slight but pleasant breeze escaped as the last ray of sunlight was dragged

over the distant mountains. A coyote, eager for
the coming night, cried once far below. Then the
twilight was silent. Silent and strangely relaxing.

Ralph spread a blanket on the ground. Not
taking off his gunbelt, he moved the holstered .45
on his hip into what he hoped would be a comfortable position. He lay down, pulled his rifle in close
to his side and turned the edge of the blanket over
the firearm, concealing it.

With tension keeping his sleep light, a foreign
sound during the early night had Richard Ralph
come abruptly awake. He lay still, waiting. There
was no sound, no indication of any movement close
to him. He was startled to see two men standing
just feet away, looking down at him. Some way
behind them stood a solitary horse. The animal
had a totally worn look, its head drooping tiredly.
The men had obviously been riding double up.

A little man with tow-coloured hair stood grinning while a tall, broad-shouldered man with
greying hair stood with his heavy plaid mackinaw
reefer open to reveal a flaming red flannel shirt.
Perspiration in the thick hairs of this man's moustache glistened in the moonlight. Either saddle
tramps or outlaws, they were both dangerous
men. Each of them had a six-gun in his right
hand. Both guns were aimed at Ralph.

'He's awake,' the big man muttered, his
swarthy face like a mask, his speech laconic.

'That's good,' the little man chuckled. 'There's
something that ain't nice about shooting a man
while he's asleep.'

Richard Ralph was pleased to detect no tremor in his own voice as he asked, 'What do you men want from me?'

'Now that ain't a nice way to speak,' the small man complained with a grin.

The big man continued. 'You ain't right hospitable, *amigo*, no fire, no coffee.'

'But that don't make no never-mind, as we ain't got time to squat and chat around a camp-fire,' the little man said. 'All we want, *muy amigo*, is the rifle we see'd you toting, your Colt and gunbelt, and that fine-looking horse of your'n. Got the Rainbow brand, I sees. If you stole that cayuse, my friend, then we'll be doing you a favour in taking it from you.'

'I didn't steal the horse,' Ralph protested.

'That's difficult to believe,' the little man shook his tow-head slowly in wonderment. 'I worked for Halleran years back and I never knowed him sell a horse.'

'Why argue about a horse that we're going to take anyway,' the big man muttered surlily.

This was what Ralph had feared since seeing the single horse that the two men had ridden up on. To be left on foot out here was a prospect too grim to be contemplated. His anxiety must have shown on his face, because the smaller man was studying him gleefully.

'It ain't right for us to worry a man like that,' the little man chuckled.

'It sure ain't,' the big man agreed. 'You explain it to him, *amigo*.'

The tow-headed man gave Ralph a broad smile.
'You won't need your horse, *compadre*. Dead men
don't ride horses.'

A wave of cold fear swept through Richard
Ralph from head to toe as he heard the double
clicks as the two men thumbed back the hammers
on their six-shooters.

It was close to midnight when Roma and Graff
entered the Pleasure Palace saloon. It was filled
with people and with noise. A fragmented grey
cloud of cigarette smoke swirled around the oil
lamps before clinging to the low ceiling. No one
paid any attention to them. The marshal carried
his rifle as usual, and his watchful slate-blue eyes
scanned the whole room in an instant. Max
Howland was at a table in a poker game with a
black-bearded cowman and a couple of young
punchers. Satisfied there was no one there who
could be a threat, Graff went with Roma to the
knife-scarred counter and ordered drinks.

With Chet Halleran securely locked away in
the isolated cabin on Rainbow's northern range,
Cado Roma had returned to town just a short
while ago. First checking on Ruth, finding her
much improved, he had gone across to the jail,
where Vern Graff had reported that all had been
quiet in town while Roma had been away.

Their drinks had just been poured when the
batwing doors behind them crashed open. The
three Slade brothers stepped in to stand looking
around. Obadiah gave a curt nod to Max Howland

at the poker table. Their presence brought a hush to the saloon.

Carrying rifles, Obadiah and Shem stood a short distance from Eli. The unarmed youngest brother's face was scratched and bruised from being dragged along the street by his horse.

Vern Graff spoke while leaning on the bar.

'If it's Chet Halleran that's on your mind, Obadiah, Wobbler Turpin's over at the jail with a scattergun. I told him to blast anyone but me who goes near the door.'

'Halleran don't interest us tonight, Marshal,' Obadiah Slade answered. 'We've come because brother Eli's got some unfinished business with Roma.'

Taking quick, short steps, Eli Slade advanced menacingly towards Roma, who stayed with his back to him, drinking his whiskey.

'Turn around, Roma,' Eli said in his subdued voice. There was a strange light glowing in his colourless eyes, and the dark scabs of unhealed wounds criss-crossed his big face.

Not turning, Roma put his right hand down to unbuckle his gunbelt. He had the belt off and was laying it on the bar when Eli made a blindingly fast move. With a speed that was astonishing in so big a man, he flung one thick arm about Roma's waist, grabbed one of Roma's legs with his other hand, and spun him upside down before slamming him hard down on to the floor.

A lancing pain shot through Roma's left shoulder as he hit the floorboards. Expecting the giant

Eli to stomp on him with both feet, Roma fought the pain and started to roll. But Eli was employing another strategy, and Roma, still bemused by being thrown so hard, felt a ponderous weight as if a horse had fallen, with him underneath.

Making full use of his heavy body, Eli Slade was lying suffocatingly on Roma, who felt himself flattening down into the blackness of a bottomless pit, which held neither sights nor sounds. The oppressive weight of Eli was still squashing him, but a feeble glimmer of light in the blackness of Roma's mind began to grow into a bright light of returning consciousness. Reaching out with his right hand, his fingers located the thick neck of Eli Slade and closed on it.

Eli struggled frantically as his supply of air was cut off. Using both hands to push himself up off Roma, his eyes seemed about to pop from their sockets, his thick tongue protruded from between his back-drawn lips, and his face was turning a dark purple. Mustering all of his immense strength, Eli jerked himself upright, breaking Roma's merciless grip on his throat.

With Eli taking in huge, choking gasps of air, Roma, who still lay upon his back on the floor, used his backside as a pivot and spun his body round. His outstretched feet, held together, caught Eli Slade behind the knees.

Seemingly suspended in the air for a long moment, Eli then crashed to the floor as Roma scrambled to his feet. Waiting for Eli to get up from the floor, Roma changed tactics when he found that his left arm hung uselessly, having been put out of action when he was slammed to the floor.

Eli Slade was on his hands and knees, shaking his head, bear-like, to clear it. Kicking out with his right foot, Roma caught the big man in his side, sending him rolling over on to his back. Taking a quick step forwards, Roma pressed the sole of his right boot into Eli's face. Keeping the pressure on hard, he twisted and turned his foot, feeling the new scabs scrunch and break up.

Seeing a long, wide, crusty scab still untouched across the big man's forehead, Roma lifted his boot to send the sharp heel in a cruelly cutting kick along the full length of the scab. Deprived of the scab that had kept it together, the skill split open and peeled redly apart.

Roma stood back as Eli got clumsily to his feet, reaching up to a flap of skin and flesh that hung down loosely over his eyes. Thinking that it was something alien sticking to his forehead, Eli tugged hard at it before realizing that it was part of his own face that he was tearing off.

Going berserk, Eli launched himself at Roma. But he was severely handicapped by the blood streaming into his eyes. Neatly sidestepping, Roma drove his right fist deep into Eli's belly, then switched it to a hook that cracked hard against the big man's jaw. It was a blow powerful enough to fell an ox, but it only caused Eli Slade to take two uncertain backward steps.

Then he was coming at Roma again, fast.

Swaying to one side, Roma had forgotten his injured shoulder, and when Eli's huge fist smashed against it the pain was so bad that Roma was close to blacking out again. He was turned by the blow so that he was facing the bar, clinging to it with his right hand to keep himself upright. Wracked with pain, his head spinning, Roma realized that his back was to Eli once again, and the big man was moving in to throw him as before.

Roma blindly lifted his right foot in a backward kick. He heard an anguished groan from Eli as the big man was backheeled in the groin. Sensing that Eli had staggered back, Roma turned to see the big man bent almost double in pain. Linking the fingers of both hands together, Roma put his hands round the back of Eli's neck. He pulled sharply down at the same time as he brought his own knee up. He felt nose and cheekbones shattering against his knee.

Eli Slade was still standing, but his face was a bloody, mutilated pulp. Breathing shudderingly and noisily, he was in danger of choking on his own blood. Roma threw a terrific right-hand punch. It landed flush in the centre of Eli Slade's ruined face. The jar of the impact travelled through Roma's arm and right down his body to his toes. He saw jagged edges of white bone poking out from the bloodied, mangled flesh of Eli's face as the big man went backwards.

Turning to say something to Vern Graff, Roma felt the saloon tilt sideways. He was attempting to get either it or himself upright, when the lights went out inside his head.

Something strange was happening to Richard Ralph as he lay looking up into the black muzzles of the two guns. A hot rage consumed him. All the injustices of the past, the dismissive way in which everyone regarded him, were running through his head. This was made worse by the confident grins of the two men. They thought they had a right to kill him; the fact that he was Richard Ralph didn't matter. Well, they were wrong. Now was when it all stopped.

Completely devoid of fear, Ralph surrendered to some strange force that welled up inside of him. It was as if he had split into two. He seemed to be two separate beings. One of him seemed to be watching the other roll sideways out of the blankets, taking his rifle with him. His action had taken the two men by surprise. Frozen in astonishment, they hadn't got around to pulling the triggers of their guns before Ralph had fired his rifle twice in quick succession.

Coming up on to his knees in a smooth movement that came naturally to him, he saw the body of the lighter man blown backwards in the night. The big man bent over slightly, and his revolver fell from his hand as he took a few faltering steps. Then his knees gave way and he sank slowly to the ground. The sound of the two shots shattering the stillness of the night had made Ralph's horse skittish. But the horse of the two men was too weary to be afraid.

Standing, rifle held at the ready, Richard Ralph walked to where the big man had fallen. The fellow lay on his face, and Ralph used the toe of his foot to roll him over on his back. At first he saw no mark on what was definitely a dead man. Then Ralph saw the dark stain on the shirt the corpse wore. Just above the waistline.

Unmoved by his first killing of human beings, Ralph walked coolly over to where the little man lay crookedly. Bending over to take a look, Ralph reeled back as he saw that his bullet, fired from low down, had entered under the man's chin to blow off the top of his head. Nothing was left of the head above the eyes and ears, and blood and brains were splattered everywhere.

Running to lean against the slender trunk of a young tree, Ralph retched noisily before vomit erupted explodingly from him.

When it was over, Ralph, his legs trembling, walked to roll up his blankets, take a refreshing swig of water from his canteen, and then saddle up. Unsaddling the dead men's horse, he took off its bridle. Slapping it hard on the flank, he hoped to send it running off into the night, into freedom. But it lacked the energy, and stayed still.

Ralph left the animal to move away in its own time. He mounted his horse and rode close to the two dead men, looking down at the bodies, completely unmoved now. Then he jabbed his horse lightly with his heels, and rode slowly down from the small hill. The self-confidence that he

had experienced before had been nothing so
profound as what he felt now. In a drastic situation, faced with long odds for survival, he had
triumphed.

His horse pressed on a little more swiftly as the
grade levelled off into a canyon. He reined it up
and leaned forward to study the rocky floor of the
canyon intersection. This wasn't an easy place to
read signs and he wasn't an expert, but the trail
was obvious. A large herd had been driven
through this winding gulch, headed toward the
north-west. It was the black hour before dawn
now, and the darkness around him was vibrating
with menace, but he rode on, totally unafraid.

Seven

When Roma regained consciousness he was sitting in a chair, bare to the waist with Doc Ferris just completing the bandaging of his left shoulder. Maggie Rumbold was fussing over him, passing him a glass of whiskey. Her presence suggested that he was in the hotel, and he looked around. They were in Maggie's private room just off the hall. Further over to Roma's right, a grim-faced Vern Graff was leaning against the glass cabinet in which Maggie kept on display her collection of Apache Indian artefacts. Roma could see his grossly swollen shoulder from the corner of his eye. Noticing this as he packed his bag, Doc Ferris gave Roma a wry smile.

'It looks bad now,' the doctor acknowledged, 'but the swelling will have gone down by tomorrow. Give it a week and it will be good as new.'

'And it will need to be,' the marshal glumly put in. Walking slowly over to stand looking down at Roma, he let a couple of minutes pass before speaking again. These minutes were marked by the grandfather clock that was too noisy in the strange quiet of the room. 'The Slades put one over on us, Cado.'

'I thought I had whupped Eli good and proper, Vern.'

The marshal nodded agreement. 'You did. But Obadiah and Shem used their young brother, Cado. While they had you giving Eli what he deserved in the Pleasure Palace, they had their hired help taking care of things elsewhere.'

'I'm not following you too good, Vern,' Roma said as he put on his shirt.

'It's like this,' Graff began. 'They checked out the jail and found Chet wasn't there.'

'So?' The pain in his shoulder stopped Roma's shrug of indifference.

'So it's real bad news I'm afraid, Cado.'

'How bad?' Roma felt sure that it was real bad.

The expression on the marshal's face convinced Roma that he was right to fear the worst. Reluctantly, very reluctantly, Graff told him.

'The Slades took Ruth.'

A distraught Maggie Rumbold was in tears as she excused herself to Roma, 'I couldn't do anything, I didn't even know about it. I had some drummers come in late off the last stage, and I must have been cooking their meal when it happened. I didn't even suspect anything until I took a hot drink up for that girl last thing, like you asked me to, mister.'

'You weren't to blame,' Roma assured the distressed woman.

Though Roma wanted to take immediate action, he remained his usual cool, calm self. In fact he was more than cool, he was cold with a terrible anger that filled his whole body. He had learned to like Ruth, to appreciate her many qualities.

'I guess the Slades will hold us to ransom, Vern.'

'That's the idea behind it,' Graff confirmed. 'They'll be offering to trade Ruth for Chet.'

'Then the answer's a simple one,' Maggie Rumbold said, uneasiness in her swift glance at the marshal. 'That girl is worth a hundred or more Chet Hallerans.'

'I hear you Maggie, and I sure wish it was as simple as that.'

Roma made a supposition. 'The Slades won't keep their side of such a bargain.'

Graff shook his head. 'They want Halleran so's they can kill him. Obadiah and Shem know they can't get away with that or anything else while I'm the town marshal.'

Roma grasped the situation. He revised his impression of Obadiah and Shem, a family solely concerned with avenging the death of a brother. They obviously had interests in things other than ranching; enterprises that were not within the law. Though they may well hate Chet Halleran, they were using their quest for vengeance as a front to get rid of a town marshal who stood in the way of their nefarious activities.

'When you go to deliver Chet, they'll use Ruth to lure you into a trap.'

'And gun me down, Cado,' the marshal said.

'You won't be on your own,' Roma promised. 'I'll be there with you.'

'The Slades will insist that I go alone to get Ruth, Cado.'

'Then we got to get Ruth now,' Roma said decisively. 'Will they be holding her at their ranch house do you reckon, Vern?'

'I'd say no. They'd expect you and me to ride out there, Cado, and they wouldn't want to face us together. The Slade boys drove a nester off his land somewhere out close to the Badlands a long while back. My guess is that they'll hold her in the nester's shack.'

'Where's that?' Roma asked as he stood, ready to get moving.

'I don't know,' the marshal admitted. 'I only heard about it once by chance. It was long before my time here in Minerva Wells.'

'Then we have to find out where it is, and get there pronto,' Roma urged.

Graff slanted a quizzical glance at the hotel owner. 'Do you recall the time the Slades moved in on that homesteader, Maggie?'

'Vaguely. Very vaguely I'm afraid, Vern. All I can remember is that the nester's name was Cox. I'm jiggered if I know where his place was at,' Maggie Rumbold said apologetically.

'Sounds to me like this is turning into council of war, so I'm going,' the doctor informed them all. 'I'll be around to do the patching up afterwards, but I want no part of violence.' He walked away from them. Pausing for a moment, he turned his head to make a suggestion. 'I know who could tell you for sure where this homestead is. Hal Halleran.'

'Halleran's at least halfway to Kansas City with the herd right now.'

'In that case,' the doctor picked up his bag and suggested, 'you might try Queenie Ralph.'

Tired and hurting from hours on the trail. Ralph rounded a rocky bend to come upon a Rainbow cowboy who was acting like a circle rider on a roundup. A relieved Ralph knew that the herd couldn't be very far ahead. Some stray steers had bedded down in deep buckrush, and the puncher had been sent back to bring them along from where they had bedded down in the long grass. As he approached, Ralph saw one steer snorting as it wheeled when the rider came into the small clearing. It came at the cowboy at a dead run, tail up and horns threatening. The rider moved out of the way. But the steer wheeled again, head down, and tried to hook the cowboy's horse. But the old, well-broken cow-horse leapt to one side so that the steer's horn missed its forepart.

Breaking away, the steer went pounding off through the high brush, heading for a flat area into which a coulee ran. This was about a half-mile away. The cowboy didn't give chase, preferring to lose one steer to all of the strays.

Though he had seen cowboys do it, Ralph had never before tried roping. Now in his new confident frame of mind he sent his horse thundering after the steer. Rope in his hand, Ralph built a loop as he rode high on his stirrups. Making his cast, Ralph lassoed the steer and brought it down.

Leaping from his saddle, he hit the ground at a run. Ralph found that reflexes he had never before put to the test were responding excellently. He had the steer hog-tied when the cowboy, a heavy-set man aged about thirty, who was a stranger to Ralph, rode up to congratulate him. 'Good work, *amigo.*'

When he and the cowboy brought the steers on to catch up with the herd, Ralph found it difficult to believe how well he had done. They passed through a valley that lay golden in the slanting rays of a setting sun. It would be cold when the sun set. Cool, purple shadows had crept far out across the flatland when Ralph and his companion crossed a ford. They heard a bellowing of cattle coming from up ahead. The herd had been bedded down for the night, and they found the Rainbow trail crew camped in the shelter of a ragged outcropping.

Impressed by Ralph's roping, and unaware of his identity, the cowboy was giving an excited account of it when Hal Halleran rode into the camp. Both astonished to see his son-in-law, and clearly having a problem in believing it *was* Richard Ralph that the puncher was talking about, the rancher reined up.

Riding his horse slowly over to face Halleran, Ralph explained why he was there. He told about

Chet shooting the saloon girl, but didn't mention that Chet had smashed him up.

'Why does that boy always have to behave like a maverick?' Halleran asked himself. 'Cado Roma came highly recommended, Richard, but he's let me down.'

'No blame lies with Roma.' Ralph put the rancher right. 'Chet had ducked out of the line shack and was in town before Roma had the chance to catch up with him.'

Grasping the horn of his saddle with both hands, reins loosely draped across the knuckles, a perplexed Hal Halleran bowed his head in thought. Then he thanked Ralph.

'You did right and you did well riding out here after me, Richard.' He took a closer look at Ralph's face. 'What happened to you, son, get kicked by a horse?'

'Something like that,' Ralph replied neutrally to pass the subject off.

Accepting this with an abstracted nod, Halleran mused. 'This has got me in a fix, Richard. What would you advise me to do, boy?'

It was indeed remarkable for Hal Halleran to ask his opinion. About to revert to giving one of his non-committal answers, Ralph remembered his new image. He saw bewilderment come into Halleran's eyes as he said in a firm voice:

'You don't have a choice, Hal. I don't give a Chinaman's cuss about what happens to Chet, but without you there he will either cause a heap more trouble, or else the judge will lock him up for

a long spell. You owe it to Queenie and her mother
to ride back with me. Ed Baker can take the herd
on.'

'You're right, son,' Halleran agreed. 'You've kind
of changed, Richard.'

'Not that I've noticed,' Ralph answered.

'Whatever, you've got it about right, boy. Give
me time to tell Ed what to do, and I'll ride back
with you.' Before reining his horse about, Hal
Halleran surveyed his son-in-law through slitted
eyes. 'I see you're wearing a gunbelt, Richard. Do
you think you could use a gun if you had to?'

'I guess we'll find out if I have to,' Ralph replied
in a quiet voice that had iron in it.

'That's the Cox shack,' Queenie Ralph told them
in a low voice.

She had insisted on accompanying them,
despite the objections voiced by Roma, Graff, and
her mother. Queenie rode a pinto, her silver-inlaid
saddle reflecting the late sunlight. She had led
Roma and Graff through the mouth of a little
gulch, which opened into a hidden valley. Queenie
was a rich man's daughter, and married, both of
which put her out of Roma's reach. But that didn't
prevent him from acknowledging that she was
beautiful and courageous.

Roma, his shoulder having rapidly returned to
normal as Doc Ferris had promised, took a look
around him in the dying light. That the Slades
favoured this place confirmed his suspicion that
the brothers' ranching business strayed outside of

the law. There were several steep approaches from this valley into the Badlands. Locations where breaks in the wall of the cliffs made possible a climb from the foothills to the craglands. This was a dangerous place to be.

They left their horses at the foot of a hogback ridge and climbed among hard, brown-stained rocks where little grass or brush grew. There was a whispering silence in the wide valley.

The sky blazed with stars and the coyotes were well tuned up. All three of them were lying at the edge of rocky ledge. The ghost of an old moon had just climbed to join the stars behind them. In its poor light, they were looking down at a sod hut. The cliffs just beyond towered over it. There was an air of utter neglect and isolation about the place, and this had Roma believing that Ruth wasn't being held here.

'Not a horse to be seen, Vern,' he remarked to the marshal.

'Don't be fooled by that,' Graff advised. 'The Slades are clever.'

'You mean they could have dropped Ruth and someone to guard her at the shack?'

'That's what I'd expect from Obadiah and Shem, Cado.'

There was just a door and one small window at the front of the shack. Suddenly the light of the moon seemed to grow brighter and Roma could see its glare reflected in shining streaks above the straggling trees that were between them and the shack. There was enough cover for Graff and himself to get close to the shack.

'How do you see this, Cado?' the marshal asked. 'We can't risk hitting Ruth by going in.'

Roma remarked; 'Which means that we have to get them out.'

A sceptical Queenie said, 'That's easier said than done. We can't even be sure that Ruth or anyone else is down there in the shack. There's no light in the window.'

Roma felt a damp night breeze against his face. Catching a brief odour of wood smoke, it seemed that the marshal was right and Ruth was being held down there.

He told his two companions, 'There's somebody in the shack. They've just lit a fire.'

'You're right, look,' Graff said with satisfaction.

Down at the shack the dull yellow glow of an oil-lamp filled the small window. It wasn't carelessness but confidence that had the Slade men give their presence away. The approach through the narrow gulch and the terrain in general meant that to attack in darkness would be an act of desperation. Roma knew that the marshal would agree to hit the unsuspecting men in the shack with a night assault.

'They aren't expecting company,' the marshal commented.

'We should give them a surprise, Vern. Do you want to call the shots?'

'The way I see it,' Graff said, 'we have to try to get them to come out one at a time.'

'Depends how many there are. I guess the first

thing to do is go down to take a look-see.' Roma signalled to the marshal by patting the sheathed knife attached to his belt.

'Right, then we know what we have to do when we get down there.'

Roma knew. As the man with a knife, he would stand against the wall of the shack close to the door. Concealed a short distance away, Graff would make small noises that would have a Slade man come out to investigate. Roma would silently knife the first man, and when he didn't go back into the shack a second would come out to look for him. It would work for up to three men, but no more. The fourth would be too suspicious to venture out.

'What if there's four or five of them, Vern?'

'Then we'll think up another plan.' The marshal then turned his head to speak to Queenie. 'You stay up here, Queenie. If me'n Roma run into trouble you ride off and leave us.'

Queenie replied with a nod. Roma and Graff went silently down the slope through the pines, their footsteps muffled by a thick carpet of wet needles. The window was too small for them to see the inside of the shack without getting close. When they were about fifteen yards away, the marshal stopped behind a tree, while Roma went on at a crouch. Reaching the shack he placed his back against the wall near the window. Stretching his neck, he took a cautious look in the unglazed window.

A tall, gangling man was standing at a stove

making coffee. The man didn't have much of a build, but he was the lean, rangy kind. Unable from that angle to see anyone else inside, Roma ducked and changed positions to come up at the other side of the window. From there, he saw Ruth sitting dejectedly on the edge of a crudely constructed bed. A second man, an elderly Mexican, sprawled dozing on a chair, his elbows resting on a table.

Carefully lifting his hand so that it was backlit by light from the window, Roma used his fingers to signal that there were two men inside. Graff answered him with a passable imitation of the cry of a night bird. Satisfied, Roma moved along the wall to stand beside the door and draw his knife. Then he waited.

A minute or so passed by, and then Graff scraped the barrel of his six-gun against the bark of the tree he was hiding behind. The sound carried in the night, and Roma heard an urgent scuffle inside the shack. The latch lifted on the door. Everything was going to plan. Then things started to go wrong. Roma held his knife at the ready, intending to move behind to clap a hand over the mouth of whoever came out, then drive his blade in close to the spine. But he had to change tactics. The lean man came out through the door and immediately sidestepped to avoid being silhouetted by the light from the door. The step took the man out of Roma's reach.

Leaping behind the gangly man, Roma gripped his man's forehead with his left hand, pulling his

head back. Bringing the knife round he slashed
the razor-sharp blade across a throat that had a
pronounced Adam's apple. To Roma's chagrin, the
man let out a yell before his jugular vein was
severed.

Roma swiftly let the dead man fall to the
ground. But it was too late. The man inside the
shack had been alerted. He called nervously, '*Que
es?*'

Not answering, Roma sheathed his knife and
drew his gun as he went cautiously back to the
window. The Mexican had his arms wrapped
round a struggling Ruth, using her as a shield
between him and the window as he shuffled
towards the door with the intention of shutting it.
Colt.45 in his hand, Roma couldn't risk a shot.

The Mexican kicked the door of the shack
closed and then manhandled Ruth back towards
the bed. She struggled, and for a few seconds her
captor's back was to Roma. The Mexican's body
blocked Ruth completely for a moment or two, but
Roma didn't fire. At such close range a bullet
could pass through the Mexican and hit Ruth.
Then Ruth was being used as a shield again, and
the Mexican alarmed Roma by calling out two
names '*Larry! Pete!*'

That meant that there had been three men.
That was a serious problem that Roma couldn't
spare time to deal with right then. Ruth's struggling had the Mexican's back towards the window
again. Having no option, Roma threw his .45 from
his right to his left hand. Drawing his knife with

his right, praying that Ruth and the Mexican wouldn't alter their positions, Roma drew back his arm and sent the knife flying in through the window.

With immense relief, he saw the blade thud deep into the Mexican's fat back. Hearing the man give a deep, rattling cough, and seeing him twist an arm behind himself in a vain attempt to pull out the knife as he slowly collapsed, Roma, remembering there was a third man, called through the window. 'Get down and stay down, Ruth. I'm coming in to get you.'

Running to the door and opening it, Roma dropped flat out of the illumination of the oil-lamp when a rifle bullet splintered the doorjamb no more than an inch from his head. He lay still, unable to reach the door to close it and shut off the light. The shot had come from Roma's left, and Graff was over to his right. The marshal called softly to him. 'Keep down, Cado. He's got you covered, and I can't get him from here.'

Roma cursed silently. He was prepared to move and have the concealed man fire again. The flash would give his location away and Graff could get him. But only if Graff had a rifle. It had been Roma's idea to leave their rifles with Queenie and the horses.

It worried him that with the door open Ruth could be a target inside the shack. If he went anywhere near the lighted doorway the rifleman could cut him down easily. Stretching out his right leg, Roma couldn't quite reach the open door with his foot. Before he could pull his foot back and form another plan of action, the concealed rifleman fired. As if struck by a club, Roma's right leg swung of its own accord, slamming against the wall of the shack. His throbbing leg convincing him that he had been hit, Roma quickly checked himself over. He was unharmed, but the unseen rifleman was good. The bullet had struck Roma's boot, tearing a section of the leather sole away.

The guy with the rifle had Vern Graff and himself pinned down. There was no way they could make a move without getting themselves killed and leaving Ruth to the mercy of the rifleman. Frustrated, he lay absolutely still in the darkness.

Eight

Ten minutes had passed since the stalemate had begun. An atmosphere of despair hung heavily in the night air. Still lying prone in front of the shack, Roma found that a dull ache had started up in his damaged shoulder. A few slight sounds led him to believe that Marshal Graff was moving stealthily and extremely slowly in the direction of the hidden rifleman. It was worrying Roma that if he could hear Graff then the concealed man must also be able to do so, when a sudden blast of the rifle proved that his concern was justified. Roma noted where the orange flash of the shot came from. The bullet tore bark from a tree where Graff must have been hiding, causing Roma to wonder if the marshal had been hit.

Then there was the sound of a second shot being fired, followed by what sounded like a body falling in the brush. This was wholly unexpected. Waiting, trying to fathom out what had happened, Roma heard Graff's cautious call.

'What do you make of that, Cado?'

Graff's call didn't draw any fire. Nevertheless, Roma waited. He was closer to the rifleman than the marshal was, and was fully exposed because there was nothing to shelter behind. To shout back to Graff would give his exact position away. With the marksmanship of the man with the rifle in mind, that would mean instant death for Roma. But then he could wait no longer.

'I reckon he could have been put out of action, Marshal.'

This theory wasn't feasible, but Roma's shout didn't draw a shot. Though aware that the rifleman could be drawing them into a trap, Roma brought himself up into a hunkering position. There was enough light coming through the open door of the shack to present him at least as a silhouette to the man with the rifle. Roma paused, motionless, expecting a shot to be fired. When after a short period nothing had happened, he ran at a crouch away from the shack. Reaching the bushes, he almost collided with the shadowy figure of Graff.

'I figure he's somewhere around the foot of that tall cottonwood,' Roma whispered.

'That's where I placed him, Cado. You move in on him from the left,' the marshal whispered, 'and I'll come from the right.'

'Watch yourself,' Roma advised. 'He's likely to see us before we get a sighting of him.'

They parted in the darkness. Moving quietly and carefully through the brush, Roma couldn't assess the situation. Then he heard rasping breathing and headed in the direction from which it was coming. He met Graff again in a small clearing where, made indistinct by moonshadows cast by the surrounding brush and trees, a man clutching a rifle was slumped. As the wheezing breathing grew louder and took on a rattle, the man's shoulders rose and fell as he struggled to get air into his lungs.

Roma and Graff were exchanging puzzled glances when a nearby noise in the brush had them twist round. Their fingers were tightening on their triggers when Graff issued out a terse command.

'Just step out without trying anything. We've both got you covered.'

They waited in a tension-filled stillness. Then they relaxed, bemused as Queenie Ralph stepped into the clearing. Her body was trembling. In a shaky voice that was close to inaudible, she asked, 'Have I killed him?'

Bending over the injured man, Roma reported, 'He's alive,' before taking away the .30-30 rifle that the man was limply holding.

Roma kicked the cartridges out of the Winchester, pumping the lever. When the magazine was empty, Roma looked at Queenie.

'You were supposed to stay up on the ridge.'

As soon as he had spoken the words, Roma realized it was a churlish thing to say. Vern Graff saw Queenie's courageous action fairly and logically.

'We should be thanking Queenie.'

'I don't want to have killed a man,' Queenie said tremulously.

'After you get to five you stop counting,' the marshal said cynically.

'I still count,' said Roma without thinking. He was aware of the amused expression on Graff's face. The marshal recognized that Roma had said this to prove to Queenie that he wasn't a callous, hardened killer.

Looking down at the shot man, who was having an even greater struggle to draw air into his lungs, Queenie anxiously asked, 'Can we take him back to town so that Doc Ferris can help him?'

'No, he's not our problem,' the marshal replied. 'We'll drop him off at the Slades' place.'

Queenie was about to argue, to protest, when the wounded man made an eerie gulping sound. Eyes opening wide, he looked beseechingly from one to another of them. Then thick dark blood erupted from his mouth, gushing out fountain-like. Bending to take a close look at the man, Roma made further discussion on the subject unnecessary when he said, 'That's it, the end. Come on, let's go down to Ruth.'

'A little while ago he was trying to kill us, Queenie,' Graff reminded her.

'But he was a person, a human being,' Queenie protested in an awed whisper.

They exchanged no further words as they neared the shack. When they were within ten feet of the open door, Roma halted them and called out the saloon girl's name. She answered faintly.

'Is that you, Cado?'

'Yes,' he replied as he led Queenie and Graff in

through the door. 'It's all over.'

She looked very ill, and was obviously weak. Helping her to her feet, Roma had to support her shaking body. She clung to Roma, her feet dragging as he gently moved her towards the door of the shack.

'We don't have a spare horse for her, Cado,' a rueful Graff said, blaming himself for the oversight.

'She's not in fit condition to sit in the saddle,' Roma said. 'She can ride up in front of me. That way I can make sure that she's all right until we get back into town.'

Disturbed by the girl's appearance, Queenie creased her brow in deep thought. She then spoke decisively.

'We'll take Ruth back to Rainbow where I can look after her.'

'You'd better think again, Queenie,' Graff wisely suggested. 'Ruth is my only witness against Chet, and your daddy won't take kindly to having her in the house.'

Dismissing this with a vehement shake of her head, Queenie said, 'I'd be the first to admit that my father can be stubborn and hard, Vern, but he is a fair man.'

'I guess you're right, Queenie.' Vern Graff quietly agreed.

'The Slades would have killed our son by now, Roma,' a worried Hal Halleran said. 'We are all indebted to you.'

It was late evening on the day that Queenie's husband and father had returned home. Roma sat in the parlour of the Rainbow ranch house with the whole family. Halleran was a generous host, and was now sharing his best whiskey with Richard Ralph and Roma. The special attention Queenie was paying him made Roma uncomfortable. It was as if he and not Ralph was her husband. Roma was conscious of Ralph's awareness of what was happening, and though Roma had not encouraged the woman, he regretted that Ralph was suffering.

'And this girl you have in the guest room?' Halleran enquired. 'You say she's the girl Chet shot?'

'She's more than that, Pa,' Queenie said. 'The Slade brothers took her captive, intending to trade her with the town marshal for Chet. Cado and Vern Graff got her back, and I said that she could stay here.'

'I wouldn't expect a kind-hearted girl like you to have done any different, Queenie.' Halleran smiled lovingly at his daughter. 'She'll be afforded every kindness while she's under my roof.'

'Thanks, Pa.'

Halleran gave a shake of his head. 'No thanks needed, Queenie. It's me who should be saying thank you, not only to you, but also to Richard who made a long, hard ride to fetch me back. I'm a lucky man to have such a family. Neither is it just family. I am also grateful to Roma.'

'Will you be going to see Judge Cronin, dear?'

Muriel Halleran asked her husband.

'Men don't come any straighter than Cain Cronin. I've known him since he was a young lawyer struggling to make a crust. Nevertheless, I won't be asking him for any favours.'

Her tired face creasing into a cobweb of age lines, Muriel Halleran turned pleading eyes to her daughter. Queenie petitioned on her mother's behalf.

'What are you saying, Pa?'

'I'm saying that I'll be doing wrong to both Chet and all of us by intervening in this,' Halleran answered. 'Don't misunderstand me. I'll see that my boy gets a fair crack of the whip. But that's as far as I'll go.'

'I don't agree, Hal,' Muriel argued, deep concern for her son lending her the courage to challenge her dominant husband. 'Without your help, Chet will go to prison for a very long time. We'll lose our son.'

'Right now we don't have a son, Muriel.'

'Do you know what you are saying, Pa?' Queenie cried.

'I know exactly what I'm saying, girl,' Halleran replied. 'It came to me while we were driving them cattle that your mother and me haven't had a son for years, if ever. Maybe punishment, a spell in prison, will be the making of Chet. If it is, then I'll welcome him as a son. Should it not be and Chet doesn't change, then I'll grieve, but neither Muriel nor myself will have lost anything. What do you have to say about that, Roma?'

'This is family stuff, Halleran. I should head on out to the barn and leave you, your wife, your daughter, and Ralph to discuss it.'

Roma noticed the grateful glance Ralph gave him for having been included, but his evasive reply had done nothing to pacify Halleran. Irritation speeded the rate of the older man's speech. 'I didn't ask for that kind of rigmarole, Roma. I want your opinion.'

'You didn't hire anything but my gun, Halleran.'

'You're a guest in my home, Roma, and this is a civilized conversation. I'd consider it polite of you to indulge an old man.'

'All I'll do,' Roma conceded grudgingly, 'if you push me, Halleran, is to give you your options as I see them.'

'That'll do me.'

'Well, you can put Chet in court and let the law take care of him. He could fetch himself something like five years in the hoosegow. A man can do a lot of growing up in five years, Halleran. You may take offence at this, but I'll say it anyway: that boy of yours has a whole heap of growing up to do.'

'You won't get no argument from me on that score, Roma,' Halleran said gruffly. 'You said options. So far you've given me just one.'

'There is another way open to you,' Roma offered.

'Then let's hear it, Roma.'

'You could send me up to the shack to turn your son loose. He could ride off somewhere and come back when his shooting of the girl has been forgotten.'

'That's what we should do, Hal,' Muriel Halleran urged her husband.

'It would work, Pa,' Queenie joined in to support her mother.

Not heeding either of the women, Halleran said to Roma, 'You're forgetting the Slades, son. They'll be here waiting whenever it is that Chet comes back.'

'Not if you hire me to take care of Obadiah, Shem and Eli, Halleran,' Roma offered.

'I'm not saying yes, Roma,' Halleran said after having given the idea considerable thought, 'neither am I saying no. Let me sleep on it. When do you ride out to fetch Chet back into town?'

'Vern Graff wants him locked up in the calaboose tomorrow night, ready for the judge the next morning. So I'll be leaving here some time before noon.'

Nodding, Halleran waited to speak until a huge grandfather clock had finished boomingly chiming midnight. Then he said, 'I'll tell you what I want you to do in the morning, Roma.'

The sky was heavy with dark cloud and there was a dampness in the air when Roma saddled up the following morning. He groaned inwardly as he saw Queenie walking his way. Huddled inside of a sheepskin coat, she had the collar turned up high. Halleran had come to the barn early that morning to give Roma his decision. He had explained

himself, perhaps excused himself, by saying what
a worry it would be to have his wild son roaming
loose somewhere.

Though Halleran had been frank with him,
Roma had sensed that the rancher had avoided
telling his family of his decision. Sure that the
approaching Queenie was coming to ask him what
her father had decided, Roma didn't know how he
would answer her.

But he found that she had other things on her
mind, and discovering what these were worried
him even more. Standing close while he tightened
the cinch, she asked a direct question.

'Whatever happens, you'll be leaving here soon,
won't you, Cado?'

He nodded as he lashed his black slicker behind
the saddle of his horse.

'Will you take me with you? Even just as far as
the nearest big town?'

Numbed by her question, Roma covered his
awkwardness by bending to lift each of the hoofs
of his horse in turn, checking the shoes.

'I don't understand, Queenie,' he said at last.

'What is there to understand, Cado?' she
enquired airily.

Over by the barn some distance away, Richard
Ralph was saddling a sleek-looking roan. He
certainly wasn't within earshot, but Roma's guilt
about the man was as real as an intense physical
pain. Roma straightened up from his task and
looked at Queenie for the first time since she had
walked up to him.

'What I don't understand is why you want to leave. This is your home. your husband and parents are here. This thing with Chet will be settled one way or another.'

'This has nothing to do with Chet,' she said. 'It's been building up in me for a long time, Cado, and you made it worse by coming here.'

Guessing that he was somehow involved, albeit not of his own volition, Roma had hoped that he was wrong. He said quietly, 'If I've done anything that causes you trouble, Queenie, then it was unintentional.'

'You've done nothing other than being you, a free spirit, which is what I want to be.'

'I'm not so free,' he said. 'I have to go where someone will pay me.'

'I understand that,' Queenie nodded, 'but you're a whole lot freer than I am. I was born into hard work on this ranch, Cado. I married at seventeen, and now my husband expects me to be a mother as well as a wife, while my parents look upon me as both a daughter and a son. I'm split in so many ways that I'm beginning to lose track of who I am. When Ruth said she was leaving Minerva Wells and I asked her where she would go, she answered that she didn't know, but if she found that the wind was in her face she would turn and go the other way. That's the kind of simple choice I've never been presented with, Cado.'

Ready to ride, one foot already in the stirrup, Roma advised, 'You seem determined to make a choice now, Queenie, but be real careful that you're making the right one.'

Swinging into the saddle, Roma was wheeling his horse round when she stepped forward to grab the bridle, bringing the horse to a halt. Her face serious, Queenie looked up at him.

'I know for sure that the right thing to do is to leave with you, Cado.'

Temptation gripped Roma. Passing years made it more and more difficult to remain a loner. Though still supremely self-sufficient when engaged in his work, he had of late been aware of an almost painful emptiness in his inactive hours. The beautiful Queenie would fill that void completely. She still held the bridle, awaiting his response. With a non-committal, 'I'll be back,' Roma touched the flanks of his horse lightly with his spurs, breaking Queenie's hold on its head. He rode away. Roma could sense a deeply unhappy Queenie standing there looking at him, but he didn't look back.

But she was on his mind as he rode beside a bountiful spring above a rock-rimmed pool with the water splashing over rocks between banks that were green with grass and brush and trees. Starting as a gorge, the valley widened out. Several miles further north would be lush meadowland that he would ride across before reaching the far-out barren wastes where he had left Chet Halleran imprisoned.

A steep narrow trail began off to Roma's left. His eye caught movement far along that trail. A rider appeared round a big outcrop. A watching

Roma was puzzled to see the rider was on a roan horse, which meant something to him. The outline of man in the saddle was familiar, too. The horse and rider came steadily on, and then Roma was even more mystified to recognize the slight, stooped figure of Richard Ralph.

Ralph rode up to him, a rifle held by one hand across the saddle horn in front of him, a strange expression on his face. He reined up when he was close. Roma waited for Ralph to speak, but the other man sat silently staring at him.

Roma eventually spoke to break the silence. 'You thinking of riding out with me, Ralph?'

'I'm not about to ride anywhere, Roma,' Ralph replied coldly. 'I came out here to give you a warning. It's about me and Queenie. I know what's going on, Roma.'

'Nothing's going on, Ralph.'

Dismissing this with a snort of disgust, Ralph said, 'Don't underestimate me, Roma.'

Had Ralph put two and two together when he had seen Queenie talking to him that morning? Roma didn't know the answer to that question, and he knew that Ralph wasn't about to tell him. He glanced up at the sun, worried about how much precious time was being wasted.

'Whatever it is eating you, Ralph,' he said, 'it will have to wait. I've got to get moving.'

As Roma pulled the head of his horse round to ride off, Ralph said in a steely voice, 'Stay away from my wife, Roma, or I'll kill you. I swear it.'

With his back to the angry Ralph, Roma rode

slowly away. Very aware that Ralph only needed
to lift his rifle and shoot him in the back, Roma
kept going. Having realized that there was much
more to Richard Ralph than anyone gave the man
credit for, Roma was pretty sure that he wouldn't
shoot him in the back.

A quarter of a mile further on, Roma's horse
climbed a steep bank. Ducking under some low
tree branches he reined up. He turned in the
saddle, and looked back. Richard Ralph hadn't
moved. He still sat tense in the saddle, staring in
Roma's direction.

Nine

A worried Vern Graff watched the three Slade brothers ride past his office and dismount in front of the Pleasure Palace. Their movements were controlled, but oddly nervous, as though they were finding it hard to maintain an appearance of studied calm. The fact that not one of the brothers ventured a glance towards the jailhouse struck the marshal as ominous. They would know that Chet Halleran was due to be brought back into town for tomorrow's court.

It was building up to being a busy night in Minerva Wells. A number of cowhands had ridden in from various ranches in the territory, and the Pleasure Palace was a buzzing mixture of sounds. Four Three Forks cowboys had ridden in, and Graff figured the Slades might use them to create a diversion.

The deliberate show of innocence on the part of the brothers warned Graff. His vigilance was strained by the need to divide it several ways. He expected Roma to ride in at any time with Chet

Halleran and was constantly looking for the first sign of them. Graff also needed to watch the hotel, where Judge Cronin had booked in, and Ruth was staying overnight. The girl had come in from the Rainbow to take her old room in readiness for the trial of Halleran in the morning.

Obadiah, Shem and Eli Slade continued to dally at the hitching rack outside ef the saloon. It was Graff's guess that they wanted to unnerve him on a night that from sun-down to sun-up would probably be the most dangerous hours of his life.

He took his rifle from the rack and stepped out into a street that had taken on a hostile atmosphere. Graff decided the best strategy would be to begin his usual nightly round by a visit to the Pleasure Palace, then walk down to the creek where no buildings fronted the street. That wide-open area marked the end of any safety Roma and Halleran might have enjoyed on the way back in. From there to the jail there were many hiding places from where a gunman could pick off passing riders.

As he stepped down from the sidewalk outside the jail to cross the street, the Slades saw him coming. Making their move seem casual, they walked towards the door of the saloon. Graff was following with his rifle held in the crook of one arm, when Maggie Rumbold came hurrying from her hotel to call to him from where she stood in the porch.

'Vernon.'

With little time to spare, Graff did no more than slow his walk.

'What is it, Maggie?'

'Ruth wants to see you.'

'I'll call in later,' Graff called, moving on.

The hotel owner refused to be put off. 'I think you should make it now, Vernon.'

Hesitating, the marshal reminded himself that the level-headed Maggie Rumbold never made a fuss about nothing. Graff turned away from the Pleasure Palace and made his way back towards Maggie.

The three riders were nearing Minerva Wells. They rode unspeaking and in single file through the twilight. Wobbler Turpin was up front, leading the horse carrying the huge Chet Halleran, whose wrists were bound together behind his back. An alert, watchful Roma brought up the rear.

Skirting the base of a brushy hill they saw the creek up ahead with the reflection from a dying sun flashing off the water like a conflagration of miniature fires. Beyond the sparkling red water was the sprawling, ugly silhouette of the town. The sound of their horses' hoofs changed for a short time as they splashed through the gravelly-bottomed creek.

Then Roma was alerted by a crimson flash of fading sunlight on metal. It came from beside the first building on their left up ahead, Halleran had seen it, too. Twisting his huge bulk in the saddle, he called back to Roma.

'At least untie my hands, Roma. Give me a chance.'

Staying silent, Roma gave a nod when Wobbler turned his head, a questioning expression on his ugly, leathery-skinned face. Roma had found Turpin to be courageous and good company. Dusk was settling fast, giving the town a look of cosiness that Roma knew was an illusion. As they approached the building on the left, Roma pulled his rifle out of its scabbard. Halleran would be the target, but a Slade wouldn't worry about whom he had to cut down to get the big man.

There was a water-trough in front of the building, and a broken-away corner of wooden sidewalk marked an entrance into a dark alleyway. Roma sensed there was someone lurking there in the darkness. His intuition had never failed him. He called a quiet warning to Turpin.

'Hold up, Wobbler.'

Rifle at the ready, Roma brought his leg over his horse in front of the saddle and slid smoothly to the ground. Crouching, he was about to run to drop down behind the trough to check out the alleyway, when a voice called out of the shadows to him.

'It's me, Cado, Vern Graff.'

'What's happening, Marshal?'

Stepping out of the total darkness of the alley, Graff lowered his voice so that the prisoner couldn't hear. He said, 'We've got ourselves a big problem, Cado. Ruth's decided that she won't give evidence against Halleran. She says that she can't do it because the Hallerans were so kind to her out at Rainbow. Do you think you can talk her round, Cado?'

'No,' Roma said. Queenie would be the reason for Ruth changing her mind. 'It wouldn't be right to try if that's how Ruth feels.'

'This is real tough, Cado. Without Ruth I'll have to turn Halleran loose.'

Roma was thoughtful. 'Maybe not. I got talking to Wobbler out at the shack. He saw enough when Ruth was shot. I reckon he would testify in court.'

'That's great,' a pleased Graff exclaimed. 'But first we need to get safely over the three hundred yards between here and my office. You and Wobbler ride up the right side of the street, keeping in the shadows. I'll walk up this side.'

'Let's hope we make it.' Roma held out his right hand.

Shaking Roma's hand, the town marshal said, 'If you and me get hit, Cado, I hope that one of us lives long enough to put a bullet in Chet Halleran.'

'That goes without saying,' a grim Roma agreed.

'I expected better from you, Queenie,' Hal Halleran said in a voice made husky by emotion.

Both of her parents had taken it badly when Queenie had nervously told them that she planned to leave the Rainbow ranch. Earlier, Richard's reaction had been to speak a name under his breath, 'Cado Roma', then give her a withering look before walking away.

Richard Ralph had been the opposite to the kind of man most folk would expect her to take up with. From the very first moment she had met Cado Roma, Queenie had been confused. Roma, a hired gun, a drifter, probably a poor catch for any woman, nevertheless was the only man she rated higher than her father.

'When will you be leaving, girl?' her father numbly asked.

'Tomorrow, after the trial.'

'Whatever happens?' Hal Halleran enquired, hoping for some kind of reassurance from her answer. Some guarantee that if he and his wife were about to lose a son, they wouldn't also lose a daughter.

'Whatever happens,' Queenie said, biting her bottom lip until it caused her pain.

Hopes dashed, a sad-faced Hal Halleran walked slowly out of the room.

The Slades made their move when the moon rode high in a cloudless sky. The town was quiet, having emptied of revellers an hour or so before. Obadiah, Shem and Eli were not going to rely on any kind of subterfuge. This was a matter of principle to them. It was the avenging of a beloved brother.

'It's started,' a tight-lipped Vern Graff called from his position by the jail's window.

They had reached the marshal's office and locked Halleran away without incident. There had

even been time to eat the bacon and beans and
drink the coffee that the amiable Wobbler Turpin
had prepared for them.

Rifle in his hand, Roma moved over to stand
beside Graff.

'What's happening, Vern?'

'See the corner of Reeve's feed store?' the
marshal asked. 'Eli's tucked himself in there.'

Scanning the street, Roma quickly studied the
irregular shadow cast by a wagon on which sacks
of feed were stacked. The shadow didn't exactly fit
the bulk it should have depicted. He said, 'There's
one of them behind that wagon, Vern.'

'I know,' the marshal nodded. 'That's Shem. I
saw him come up.'

A slight movement caught Roma's eye. It was
no more than a blurred alteration on the edge of a
pool of shadow. But it was enough. Roma placed
the third Slade brother.

'Obadiah's in the doorway of the bank, across
the street from his brothers.'

'Ah,' Graff gave a grunt of satisfaction. 'I was
wondering where he was holed up.'

'You're real good, Cado.' Wobbler, who was on
the far side of the window peering out, compli-
mented Roma.

'Not good enough to figure out why they're not
making a move,' Roma said.

'That's puzzling me,' Graff admitted. 'They're
not close enough to hit us hard.'

Four cowboys had come staggering out of the
Pleasure Palace. Reeling, they made their way to

the hitching rail. Shouting, laughing and singing, they swung drunkenly up into their saddles. They had the appearance of a quartet of revellers happily ending a good night by heading back to the ranch. But Roma could sense the increase in tension that the sight of them brought to Graff.

'Three Forks men?' he asked sharply.

'That's right,' the marshal replied. 'And it's my guess that they are not as drunk as they want us to think.'

Silently agreeing, Roma watched the four men intently. Their drunken movements were exaggerated, and he, like Graff, was expecting trouble of some kind from them. But they wheeled their mounts away from the rail and spurred them down the street, four abreast.

Whooping and hollering, they went on their way before drawing six-shooters and firing into the air. This was customary behaviour with drunken cowpokes, but the four of them went quiet and reined up when they reached Maggie Rumbold's hotel.

'They're dismounting,' Wobbler warned his companions.

The four riders hitched their horses then jumped up on the wooden sidewalk. No longer drunk, they hurried towards the hotel doorway.

'Ruth!' Roma uttered the name tersely. 'We have to get over there, Vern.'

'The Slade boys would catch you in their crossfire,' an anxious Wobbler warned.

'It could be a decoy. You stay here to see they

don't get Halleran, Vern,' Roma said.

'One man couldn't do it,' the marshal objected. 'We have to go down that street blasting left and right, Cado. That's the only way; to force Obadiah, Shem and Eli to keep their heads down. When I give the word, Wobbler, yank the door open. As soon as me and Cado's outside, shut the door and fix it. Use that scattergun if a Slade gets near enough. We'll be back.'

'I sure hope so, but I doubt it,' Wobbler Turpin said soberly.

On Graff's word of command the two of them went out through the door fast. The three Slade brothers immediately opened up with rifles. About six feet apart, running parallel, Roma and Graff went down the street, firing their rifles from the hip. Lead sang and whistled around them. Roma heard the whine of a ricochet, and he was aware of Graff faltering. Then the marshal went down on to his knees. Roma forced himself to keep going. If Graff wasn't dead, then he would need help. But saving Ruth was Roma's priority.

Running on in a straight line, knowing that zigzagging would serve no purpose in this situation, Roma thought he caught the sound of running footsteps catching up with him. He believed that his ears, ringing from his own and the Slades' rifle fire, were playing tricks on him. But then a rifle blasted away from close by, and he knew that Graff was back up on his feet and running.

As they neared the hotel, the sound of gunfire

had brought two of the four cowboys back out on
to the sidewalk. They were looking around, trying
to assess the noisy gun battle in the moonlight.
With neither the time nor the inclination to be
merciful, Roma and Graff turned their rifles from
where the Slades lay hidden in the shadows, to
the pair of cowpunchers.

One of the cowboys folded double instantly,
coughing blood as he sank to his knees and then
rolled over to lie still. The second man ran for his
horse, tugging in an effort to free the reins from
the hitching rail. Roma fired, but the man had
moved suddenly and his horse caught the slug.
Screaming in agony, it reared up, snapping the
rail and pulling it away. There was pandemonium
as the other three horses panicked and reared
before galloping away together, their reins still
tied to the broken rail that they pulled along the
street.

The cowboy was reaching up to swing from the
bridle of his shrieking horse in an effort to pull
the animal on to all four hoofs. Mortally wounded,
the horse reared even further, going over backwards with the cowboy still holding on to its head.
Roma saw the cowpoke's legs flailing the air. Then
the puncher lost his grip and fell to the ground.
With a dying, gurgling scream, the horse crashed
down on top of its rider. The cowboy gave a
muffled half cry, half groan, as his ribs were
crushed and his bones broken.

The marshal and Roma went crashing in
through the door of the hotel together.

'Ruth's on the first floor, last door on the right,' Roma panted as they ran for the stairs and reached the first landing.

A figure moved up ahead. It was one of the Three Forks cowboys. He had a six-shooter in his hand, but he was no fighting man. Moving awkwardly on a cowboy's bent legs, he turned to release a shot at Roma and Graff. The bullet went wide, but Roma squeezed the trigger of his rifle and the slug tore most of the cowpuncher's face away. The force of the bullet swung him round, his shattered face splattering the wall red and smearing blood down it as he slid to the landing, dead.

'Three down, one to go,' Graff muttered grimly.

Then a noise down in the hall had them both running back for the stairs. They jumped down them three at a time as they saw the last of the four cowboys come out of a back room and dash for the door.

Unable to get a shot at him, they followed him out of the hotel. Outside, bewildered by the discovery that his horse was gone, and shaken by the sight of his friend squashed flat under a dead horse, the cowboy was running this way and that in panic. He swung round at them with time only to point his .45 before a bullet from Graff's rifle slammed into his chest and sent him flying to land on his back in the street.

'Wobbler and Halleran!' Graff shouted to Roma as the sound of shots came from the direction of the jail. The marshal was bleeding from the left temple. Roma guessed it had been a ricochet, a flattened bullet, that had stunned Graff, knocking him down.

They ran back the way they had come. A heavy booming sound had the marshal calling to Roma. 'That's Wobbler's scattergun.'

There were two figures at the door of the jail, kicking it open as Roma and Graff ran up, expecting to hear a second blast from Wobbler. There was nothing. Lying in the dust in front of them, making whimpering sounds, was Eli Slade. His left arm was all but severed from the shoulder, ripped away by a blast from Wobbler's scattergun. He was bleeding to death.

Together they launched themselves at the jail door as the two Slade brothers were struggling to close it. The force with which Roma and the marshal's shoulders impacted upon the door sent Obadiah and Shem Slade staggering backwards off balance. Obadiah was on one knee reaching for the rifle he had dropped. Roma swung the butt of his rifle up to catch him under the chin. Head going back, an ugly grimace twisted Obadiah's face as a surprisingly loud snapping, cracking sound signalled that the blow had broken his neck.

Shem Slade was standing facing them with his back against the wall, holding his rifle by the barrel, the butt of the weapon resting on the ground. His usual friendly smile was on his face, and he said, 'Well, well,' in the way he would have greeted Roma and Graff had they been unexpected but more than welcome guests.

Both Roma and Graff had him covered with their rifles. Graff said, 'Either drop the rifle or make your play, Shem.'

'Believe it or not, Marshal,' Shem Slade said conversationally, 'I abhor violence such as this.'

'Let go of the rifle and there'll be no more violence, Shem,' Graff said.

'What then?' Shem Slade said with a sad smile as he stared down at his brother, who lay with his head twisted at a grotesque angle. He looked up at the marshal. 'And what of young Eli, Vern, did you see him outside?'

'We saw him, Shem.'

'Dead, Marshal?'

'Probably. If not, it's only a matter of minutes,' the marshal replied.

'First Noah, now Obadiah and Eli.' Shem gave his head a little sorrowful shake. 'What is there left for me, Marshal?'

'You have the ranch, and . . .' Graff started to say, but broke off as a smiling Shem brought his rifle up fast.

The shots fired by Graff and Roma were close to simultaneous. Both slugs hit the last surviving Slade, spinning him round and round until he crashed against a wall and bounced off to slam face down on the floor.

When the smoke cleared a little, Vern Graff coughed as the acrid smell of cordite affected his throat; then he said glumly, 'I don't think Shem was going to shoot us, Cado.'

'No,' Roma agreed. 'I guess we done what he

wanted, put him out of his misery.'

'It's a nasty world,' the marshal said hollowly.

'It gets nastier, Vern,' said Roma, as he caught sight of Wobbler Turpin's body crumpled up in a corner. The little man's eyes were staring into eternity, and the front of his shirt was soaked with blood.

'There goes our only witness,' the marshal said callously.

Roma recognized that Graff's tough comment was a cover for the sorrow he felt over Wobbler's death. Roma was emotionally moved, too, possibly more so. The small man had made a great companion.

'What's going on out there?' Chet Halleran's voice, made shaky by apprehension and fear, called from the cages at the rear of the building. Roma and Graff exchanged dull-eyed glances. The irresponsible Halleran, who had caused the shooting and the dying, had survived. Natural justice had failed, and now, with Ruth refusing to testify and Wobbler dead, it was an odds-on bet that man-made justice would also be ineffectual.

Ten

The sensation caused by the deaths of the three Slade brothers, Wobbler Turpin, and the Three Forks cowboys made the release of Chet Halleran less of an anticlimax than it should have been for the town. Cain Cronin, the judge, had declared there was no evidence on which to hold Halleran for trial. Hearing this, the folk of Minerva Wells went about their business. The killing was over and would soon slip unnoticed into the history of a violent territory. Only those involved remained caught up in the tail end of the Halleran drama.

Standing outside the jail with Vern Graff, Roma saw Queenie and Ruth with Hal Halleran, waiting for Chet to come out of the schoolhouse that had been used as a court. The pair of them seemed bemused rather than worried. Roma had known other decent families plagued by an uncontrollable son or daughter. Both Hal Halleran and his daughter would be only too well aware that the release of Chet by the law on this occasion was not the end of anything. It was just yet another beginning in the big man's turbulent life.

Judge Cronin had kept Chet back for a lecture about his behaviour. Though he must have known that he was wasting his time, nevertheless, the judge insisted on going through the motions. Roma and Graff had left the huge young man in the building, looking humble and contrite for the judge. It had been an act on Chet's part, and Graff commented on it now.

'Cronin may as well be talking to that prize Jersey cow old Hal keeps out at Rainbow, Cado.'

'What of Chet now, Vern?' Roma asked.

'He'll be right peaceful,' Graff answered, 'until the next drink, the next woman, or the next argument.

'Which won't be long in coming.'

Graff shook his head. 'If Hal and Queenie can't get the boy to ride out to the ranch with them, then in less than an hour he'll be causing mayhem. What will you be doing, Cado, staying here to keep a tight rein on Chet?'

'I guess not,' a rueful Roma answered. 'I reckon I'll ride out to Rainbow and collect the money due to me, then head off back to Santa Fe.'

'I'll be sorry to see you go, Cado, but you're a man always drawn to what's beyond the next hill. I wouldn't try keeping you here, but I reckon that's not how others might feel.'

'You trying to tell me something, Marshal?' Roma asked.

'You don't need telling, Cado,' the marshal said

with a tight little grin that had little humour to it.
'I'd say you're going to find it difficult to shake
Queenie off.'

'You're good at reading signs, Vern.'

'That's how I've managed to stay alive.' Graff
grinned, humorously this time. 'Queenie was disil-
lusioned with everything here before you rode in.
Do you want to shake her off, Cado?'

Looking over to where Queenie was engaged in
conversation with Ruth, Roma had no answer for
the marshal. Probably Queenie was everything that
he had ever wanted. But there were far too many
complications for it to work out between Queenie
and him. Perhaps he was the largest obstacle.
Having only ever known one way of life, as a loner,
he doubted that he could adapt. In a way, he
dreaded going out to the ranch to collect his money
from Hal Halleran. It would be real awkward if
Queenie was still of a mind to ride off with him.

'Here he comes,' the marshal said.

Chet Halleran came out of the schoolhouse.
Shutting the door behind him, he stretched his
arms above his head and expanded his chest as he
breathed in deeply. Dropping his arms, he looked
across at Roma and Graff, scowled and then looked
away. Then he spotted his father and sister and
walked over to them. Roma saw Ruth hurry away
before Chet reached the two people she had been
with.

'Hardly a happy reunion,' Roma remarked as
Chet Halleran ignored the hand that his father
extended.

'There's nothing happy when Chet Halleran is around,' Vern Graff said.

Seeing the hurt on her father's face as he withdrew the hand Chet had ignored, Queenie felt a mixture of sadness and fury. Her brother never showed any kindness, even accidentally. His release on the shooting charge was a fluke and no cause for celebration. It would have been better for all concerned, her parents in particular, if Chet had gone to prison for a long time.

Whatever he did now was sure to cause trouble. He made her feel guilty about planning to leave; abandoning their parents in what was their fast-approaching hour of need. If Chet went back to the ranch, then she felt it a duty to be there to protect her parents. If he didn't go back, then she should be at the Rainbow to console her mother and father, both of whom would be upset if Chet didn't return home. Whatever happened, her brother was now either directly or indirectly responsible for the deaths of four Slade brothers in total, as well as poor Wobbler Turpin and the Three Forks employees who had been caught up in it all. Doubtless those deaths weren't troubling Chet's conscience, but they would weigh heavily on her parents and herself for the rest of their lives.

Richard had been avoiding her ever since she had told him she was going away. At the Rainbow they hadn't known that Chet would escape trial that morning. Her mother had remained at the ranch to spend the day worrying about how bad would be the news they brought back. Queenie had expected her husband to ride in with her father and her, but there had been no sign of Richard when they had left.

The way Queenie saw it she would sacrifice her last chance of happiness in life if she remained at home. Ruth, whose companionship had come to mean a lot to Queenie, had said a half-goodbye before rushing off to avoid Chet. As Ruth was intending to leave on the stage that afternoon it was unlikely that Queenie would ever see her again. That thought produced an aching emptiness deep inside of her. It was a hole that was growing fast. Queenie felt that there would soon be nothing of her left but that hole if she didn't get away from Minerva Wells.

Seeing Cado Roma across the street was both thrilling and unsettling for Queenie. Roma and Vern Graff had become close friends. But neither friendship nor anything else would keep a man like Cado Roma in one place for any length of time. He, too, would be gone before that day was out. For her to stay behind would mean suffering a terrible loneliness.

'If you ride out with me and your sister now, son,' Hal Halleran was saying, 'you and me can leave before sundown and catch up with the drive. I'd be a proud man riding into Kansas City with my son at my side.'

Thinking, Chet tilted his head to one side. 'I reckon as how I'd like me to take a look at Kansas City. You got yourself a deal, Pa.'

The pleasure and relief her father showed made Queenie's heart go out to him. Slapping his son on the shoulder, he said, 'That's real good news, Chet. Vern Graff says he put your horse in Ed Holley's livery. Me 'n Queenie will go down there with you, then we'll all ride home together.'

'No.'

The one word spoken flatly by her brother chilled Queenie. It had the ring of the old Chet behind it, and from experience she knew that he had plans other than the one he had agreed with his father. Hal Halleran was about to be bitterly disappointed yet again by his wayward son. She knew she had it right when she heard Chet continue to speak.

'You and Queenie ride on out, Pa,' he said affably. 'I've had it rough these past few weeks, and I've got to have me a drink. I'll follow on, be there within an hour.'

All three of them knew that he was lying, but only Chet could be content with the lie. Hal Halleran looked devastated, and Queenie felt physically sick. Halleran history was about to repeat itself, as it always did over and over again, because of Chet. Once her brother went into the Pleasure Palace, one drink wouldn't be enough. One or another of the saloon girls would become the focus of his attention. For him the girl would take on an additional loveliness with every drink he poured down his throat. If he came home at all, it wouldn't be until gone midnight, and then he would be in a drunken state. He would probably make it out to the Rainbow then, if he didn't fall from his horse and sleep the rest of the night away in a ditch. That would be nothing new for Chet. But, whatever happened, he certainly would be in no fit condition to go on the trail with his father.

'I don't think that's a good idea, Chet . . .' Queenie's father started to say, but broke off, his face crumpling because his son was already walking away.

They watched him go across the street. There was belligerence in his walk, and the swing of his wide shoulders was a reminder that he was physically powerful enough to finish whatever he might start in the way of trouble. The father and daughter watched his broad back until he went in through the door of Max Howland's Pleasure Palace.

'Come on, Pa,' Queenie said sympathetically then, putting a hand on her father's arm. 'Chet won't be far behind us.'

Now she was lying, but Queenie excused herself because of her good intentions. It depressed her terribly to realize how often she had been in this situation before. She was a cushion between her brother and her parents. Absorbing the shocks from Chet, she made it more comfortable for them. Yet that meant that it was always she who took the strain, and that strain was becoming intolerable.

Both of them feeling too low in spirit to make small talk, Queenie and her father mounted up and rode slowly out of town. Each of them was lost in their own dreary thoughts. Being in Chet's company was not pleasant, but it was preferable to worrying over where he might be and what trouble he might be getting involved in. Both of them were fearful of what the rest of the day might bring. It had never been plainer to Queenie that it was Chet who would decide what was to happen in the hours to come. Chet had been in charge of their lives since he had reached the age of fifteen or sixteen, and would continue to run their lives in the foreseeable future.

She wondered if her father had realized this. Queenie was pretty sure that if this had occurred to Hal Halleran he would have pushed it from his mind before it could gain a hold. Both her father and her mother had a blind spot, a deliberate one she was certain, where her brother was concerned. With that in mind, Queenie felt she would be doing them a favour by leaving. Left on their own, her parents would be forced to see what Chet really was, then they would come to terms with it.

They made their way back to the ranch along the lower trail. As they skirted an entanglement of fallen trees, Queenie leaned over in the saddle to pull a stalk of wild wheat out of its coarse scabbard and was chewing on the sweet end when she heard the steady thud of the hoofs of a horse being ridden at a leisurely gait. Above them on a trail the figure of a rider moved across her line of sight. It was no more than a brown shadow that was quickly gone. But she had recognized her husband. He was heading in the direction of town where Chet would have already started on a drinking spree.

Queenie was alarmed, but nowhere near as much as her father was. When she said, 'That was Richard, wasn't it?' Hal Halleran was already reining his horse about and jabbing in the spurs to head back the way they had just come.

'What's the matter, Pa?' she yelled as she sent her horse in a gallop after him.

'Didn't you see, Queenie?' her father answered her with a question of his own. There was anxiety etched deep in the lines of his weather-beaten face.

'See what?' Queenie had to shout because Hal Halleran was moving ahead of her. The answer he called back made it seem that an icy hand had gripped her heart.

'Richard was wearing a gunbelt.'

Having said his farewells to Marshal Vern Graff, Roma was about to mount up to ride out to the Rainbow Ranch before leaving, when a startled exclamation from the normally unexcitable Graff stopped him.

'What have we here!'

Roma was as surprised as the marshal to see a resolute-looking Richard Ralph riding towards them. As he got down from the saddle, they could see that Ralph was wearing a gunbelt and low-slung holstered Colt .44. Somehow, the gunslinger's armoury and the meek Richard Ralph didn't go together. Never of an impressive appearance, Ralph was a ludicrous figure now as he hitched his horse to the rail outside the marshal's office and came towards where Roma and Graff now stood side by side.

'Where's Halleran, Marshal?' a bland-faced Ralph asked.

Looking past him to the far end of the street Graff screwed up his eyes, then said, 'That looks to me like Queenie and her father riding in now, Richard.'

'It's Chet I'm looking for.'

Hearing this from Ralph, Roma and Graff exchanged glances. Both of them were well aware of what had happened the last time that Ralph had gone looking for Chet Halleran. Roma raised a quizzical eyebrow at the marshal, who gave him an almost imperceptible shrug in return.

'Last I saw of Chet he was going in Max Howland's place,' Graff said, adding in a drawl, 'Tell me you ain't about to go looking for him, Richard.'

'No,' Ralph assured the marshal with an emphatic shake of his head. 'I'm asking you to go in the Pleasure Palace and tell Halleran I'll be out here in the street waiting for him. I'm calling him, Marshal.'

'You can't be thinking straight, Richard,' a bewildered Graff protested.

'I know my own mind, Marshal, believe me. Go tell Chet that I'm waiting.'

'What do I do, Cado?' Vern Graff pleaded, finding himself in a situation that, for the first time in his life, had him beat.

'I guess that you'd best do as the man wants, Vern.'

A far from happy Graff walked off in the direction of the saloon. When he was half-way across the street, Hal Halleran and his daughter reined up beside him. Graff spoke to them gruffly.

'Ride back up the street a ways, Hal, Queenie. There's going to be gunplay.'

The Hallerans looked across to where Richard Ralph stood apart from Cado Roma. Hal Halleran asked, 'What's going on here, Vern?'

'Ralph's calling Chet out, Hal.'

'Good God!' Halleran exclaimed. 'You have to stop this, Vern.'

Graff spread both hands in a gesture of apology. 'You know I can't do that, Hal. As long as it's a fair fight, the law doesn't permit me to interfere.'

'How can it be a fair fight, with Richard up against the likes of my brother?' Queenie, her body trembling, close to tears, enquired plaintively.

'That's not unfair, Queenie, but unequal, which has no standing in law. All I can do is make sure that nothing unlawful takes place. I'm sorry.'

With that, Graff carried on towards the Pleasure Palace. The Halleran father and daughter sat motionless for a short time, undecided. Then they turned their horses, rode several yards back up the street, and dismounted outside of the general store that Richard Ralph's parents had once kept.

When the town marshal returned to where Roma and Ralph stood, the latter walked to meet him, asking, 'Well?'

'Chet will be out in a few minutes,' Graff replied, then walked on to where Roma waited.

'How did Chet take it?' Roma asked.

'He was still laughing when I left him, Cado,' the marshal replied. 'Whatever happens, neither you nor I mix in this unless Chet tries something.'

'Facing Ralph he won't need to try anything,' Roma said glumly, noticing the air of expectation that was now gripping the street.

Queenie and her father were the most worried, but they were not the only ones watching and waiting. From windows, doorways, and safe distances an audience of townsfolk was poised for what promised to be a dramatic event.

Richard Ralph had walked past the saloon before turning and waiting some twenty yards up the street. Roma had never seen so incongruous a gunman. His body made stiff by tension had him look like a child play-acting. The building situation should be nipped in the bud. It was morally murder to permit Ralph to face Chet Halleran, but Roma could not interfere. There was, as Town Marshal Graff had pointed out, no law against it.

There was a concerted, audible gasp then as a smiling Chet Halleran came out of the Pleasure Palace. Remaining on the sidewalk to stare at Ralph for a few moments, he chuckled, shaking his head slowly in amazement, then stepped down to the street. Walking away from Ralph for a short distance, he then turned to face him. Supreme confidence was evident in his stance. The stark contrast between the two men brought despair to the watching people. The town had gone very quiet; an eerie silence that was broken just once as

Queenie Ralph called beseechingly but vainly, 'No, Richard! No!'

The two men had begun walking slowly towards each other when Max Howland came out of his saloon, carrying a rifle. With the weapon pointed at Richard Ralph, the saloon owner said threateningly, 'Go home, Ralph. I won't stand by and see this young man caused further trouble. Because you're married to his sister, Chet won't want to kill you, but I'll do it for him if you don't vamoose, pronto.'

Roma heard Vern Graff cynically say under his breath, 'Chet's more likely to kill that kid because he is married to his sister.' Then he said aloud to Roma. 'You stay out of it, Cado, but I've got to take a hand in it now that Howland's dealt himself in.'

But before the marshal could intervene, the street exploded into unexpected action. Drawing his Colt at a speed that caused most of the watchers to miss the move, Ralph fanned the hammer with his left hand to send a shot at Max Howland. It was the smooth and competent action of a veteran gunslinger. The stock of Howland's rifle shattered; long splinters of the wood ripping open the saloon-keeper's right arm. Instantly dropping the broken weapon to the sidewalk, an ashen-faced Howland staggered back towards the door of his premises, holding his shattered arm.

By that time, Ralph had slid his gun neatly back into its holster and was advancing on a suddenly deflated Chet Halleran, deliberately pacing his slow walk so that it took on a menace of its own.

'Where did Ralph learn to shoot like that?' an incredulous Graff gasped.

'Looks to me like it came natural to him,' Roma opined. 'It's rare, but not unknown. I've had a few unlikely looking *hombres* surprise me in my day.'

'So have I,' the marshal admitted, before going on as disbelieving as before. 'But Richard Ralph!'

By then, Ralph was close to Chet Halleran, facing him with a confident look on his gaunt face. His right arm was held out from his body, his open hand hovering over the handle of his holstered .45. He spat out his words.

'It's up to you, Halleran. Draw when you're ready.'

With uncertainty twitching at his grin until it turned into a grimace, Chet Halleran seemed about to go for his gun, but he hesitated. Roma saw that as a bad sign, and said so to Graff, who nodded agreement. Then they noticed that Chet could no longer hold his brother-in-law's steady gaze. He averted his eyes.

Ralph taunted him. 'You're yellow, Halleran. I always thought you were more coyote than the mountain-lion you believed yourself to be. Draw, you skulking sidewinder, draw!'

Halleran was plainly riled, and for a moment it seemed certain that he would go for his gun. He looked sullenly at Ralph, who drew his .45 at lightning speed, fired a shot that kicked up a little fountain of dust between Chet Halleran's feet, and had the Colt back in its holster before Halleran had landed from a startled jump in the air.

'Make your move, big man!' Ralph shouted, his voice echoing on a street that was silent in the grip of a stifling tension.

Still appearing as if he might draw, Chet Halleran suddenly spun on one heel and walked away from Ralph. Roma watched him go, head resting down on his barrel-chest in shame, the huge, muscular, powerful body pathetically slumped. As he passed where his father and sister stood, Hal Halleran looked at him with a disgust that bordered on contempt.

For a long time, Richard Ralph stood staring at the back of the man whose nerve he had broken. Then he gave a curt nod, as if agreeing with something that was going on inside his own head, and walked down to untie his horse from the rail. Though just feet away from Roma and Graff, he totally ignored them. Mounting up, he rode out of town, his horse at walking pace; as he passed his wife and father-in-law, he dismissed them in the same offhand way as he had Roma and Graff.

At the far end of the street, Chet Halleran had disappeared into the livery stable, obviously to fetch his horse.

Roma remarked to Graff. 'I guess that's the last you'll ever see of Chet Halleran in Minerva Wells, Vern.'

'That's for sure,' the marshal agreed.

A reluctance to arrive at the Rainbow caused Roma to ride slowly out from town. He recognized that he was being foolish, that he would have to face the

Hallerans at some time, but he couldn't prevent himself from delaying the inevitable. It surprised him to find how difficult it had been to say goodbye to Ruth. Packing her bag in the hotel room, Ruth had briefly hugged him to her, and her eyes had been brimming with tears when she released Roma. He had hurried from the room and down to where he had tied his horse to the rail outside.

Had he not needed the money so badly, he would have probably ridden off then without any further involvement. As he rode closer to the Rainbow, it eased his worry to see that there was no one around outside the house. With luck, he would be able to pick up what was owed to him and get away without encountering Queenie.

Getting off his horse in a deserted yard, he walked round the corner of the house and up the steps to rap with his knuckles on the front door. There came the sounds of someone stirring inside. After a long interval, which seemed to be an interminable time for Roma, a morose Hal Halleran opened the door. He looked haggard; at least ten years older than when Roma had last seen him.

'Oh, it's you, Roma,' the rancher greeted him. 'You're on your way then, son. I won't pretend that it went how I'd hoped it would, but you earned your money. Come on in and I'll settle with you.'

Roma followed Halleran into a well-furnished parlour, and took the chair that the rancher gestured him towards. The full upholstery of the armchair embraced him as he sat. It was the ultimate in comfort, but Roma found the way it held him embarrassing. There was a large painting in an ornate golden frame hanging on the wall opposite to where he sat. A roll-top writing desk looked to Roma to be a very expensive item. This was a strange world that he knew nothing of. It was alien to him, and made him ill at ease.

Able to hear movement in a nearby room, he guessed that it was Muriel Halleran. He hoped that it was not Queenie Ralph. He moved to the edge of the seat as Halleran got a black tin box from a cupboard. With the uncharacteristic movements of a weary old man, the rancher sat at the table and started to count money out, talking miserably as he did so.

'It was none of your doing, Roma, but at least I now have got it straight about Chet.'

'He'll be back, Halleran,' Roma said, though he didn't believe his own words. 'Once all that has happened is in the past, forgotten, your son will come riding in one day.'

Looking at him through eyes that said he hadn't slept for a long time, Hal Halleran said, 'If that boy came back, I'd straight away run him off my land.'

'Perhaps not, Halleran. Don't they say something about blood being thicker than water?'

Dismissing this suggestion with a scowl, Hal Halleran said, 'I can't believe that boy has either Muriel's or my blood in his veins, Roma. Why couldn't it have been the other way around, with Chet being strong and straight the way his sister is?'

'Then you wouldn't have a fine daughter like Queenie,' Roma pointed out.

'That's true,' Halleran agreed. 'If you want to stay on here at the Rainbow, Roma, you can name your own wages.'

'You've just paid me a compliment, Halleran, but you can't buy yourself a son.'

'It would be a better world if you could,' Halleran complained. 'That way you could choose exactly what you want.'

'Have faith, Halleran. Your son will come home.'

'I have no son now.'

The old man's voice was in danger of cracking as he said the last sentence. Feeling awkward, Roma stood and took the money Halleran held out to him. The rancher guided him to the front door as if Roma had been a dinner guest. Coming out on to the veranda, Halleran offered his hand and Roma shook it.

'I'm sorry about the way things worked out, Halleran.'

'Perhaps it's for the best, son,' Halleran said with a shrug. 'I've been fooling myself all these years, not wanting to see the truth. Whatever might happen now, I want you to know that I don't hold you responsible in any way, son.'

Unable to understand what the rancher meant, Roma's imagination worked overtime and he feared the worst. He knew that he needed to get out of here fast before Queenie had the chance to complicate his life irrevocably. There was an urge in him to ask Halleran to explain what he had said, but the rancher gave him no time.

Releasing Roma's hand, Halleran went on, 'If

you're passing this way again, Roma, call in. You'll be sure of a welcome.'

Both of them knew that this was said out of civility and was not really an invitation.

Roma went along with the lie because it was the polite thing to do.

'I'll sure do that, Halleran.'

Walking away, Roma rounded the corner and saw another horse ground-hitched close to his. There was someone standing on the other side of the horse. Roma could see legs but couldn't tell who it was. As he went round his horse his breath escaped in a mighty rush, a silent sigh. Queenie Ralph was standing beside the other horse, strapping a large bag behind the saddle. Roma tried to drag air into his lungs, but his chest refused to expand. Shock seemed to have paralysed his whole system.

Unsmiling, Queenie turned her head to him.

'Like I said, Cado. Just as far as the next town, if that's the way you want it to be.'

Roma didn't know how he wanted it to be. He couldn't deny the feelings he had for this lovely girl, but right then he just needed to get away from there. Sensing that he and Queenie were being watched, Roma looked behind him. Hal and Muriel Halleran had come round the corner of the house to stand watching them. The elderly couple looked terribly sad. They clung to each other as if stood on the deck of a sinking riverboat.

Recovering, Roma said, 'I'm used to riding fast, far, and alone, Queenie. Your life is here, at the Rainbow.'

'No.' Her tone adamant, she came round her horse to stand close to him. 'Nothing you say will stop me . . .' she was saying when she broke off. Queenie had been looking past him over his shoulder, and Roma saw her eyes cloud. He swung his head round to see Richard Ralph walking lithely towards them. He was wearing a gunbelt.

'Step away from her, Roma.'

For her own safety, Roma pushed Queenie away. He misjudged his strength, causing her to stagger and come close to falling. He said to Ralph, 'There's no call for gunplay here, Ralph.'

Coming to a halt about six feet from Roma, Ralph told him, 'There'll be no gunplay, Roma. You aren't Chet Halleran. If I draw on a professional gunslinger I'll be dead.' Putting a hand carefully to the buckle of his gunbelt, he undid it and let the belt and its holstered gun drop to the ground. 'I'd bet anything that you aren't so good when you're not behind a gun.'

Aware that he was being pushed into a fistfight, a resigned Roma unbuckled his gunbelt and reached up to lay it across his saddle. Before he could turn back to face him, Richard Ralph caught Roma with a blow behind his right ear. Stunned for a moment, Roma clutched the girth of his saddle with his left hand to steady himself. Sensing Ralph moving in on him, he drove his right elbow back hard. He felt the elbow bury itself deep in the other man's midriff. Swiftly swinging round, Roma sent a hard right-hand punch to Ralph's jaw. The blow landed solidly, knocking the smaller man off his feet, sending him flying backwards.

As far as Roma was concerned, that would be the end of it. But when Ralph's shoulders touched the ground, he somehow used them as a spring to send himself back upright. Coming up like an acrobat, Ralph landed on his feet. The superb movement took Roma so much by surprise that Ralph was able to catch him with a left and right to the face. The lightly built Ralph was amazingly fast. Both punches were stinging rather than heavy, but Ralph's right-hand punch opened up Roma's left cheek.

Feeling warm blood running down his face, Roma took the fight seriously for the first time. Sidestepping as Ralph came at him again, he drove his right fist hard into Ralph's body. Staggering back, Ralph was having difficulty in breathing. He was struggling to inhale, and when he did there was an awful wheezing rattle. Crying out his name, Queenie ran to him but, though doubled over, he pushed her away with a thrust of his arm.

'Don't hit him again, Roma,' Queenie pleaded. 'Richard's ill, really ill.'

Ralph, bent over and gasping for breath, was obviously distressed. Even without Queenie's plea, Roma would not have taken advantage of his sick opponent. He lowered his arms as she called. That was a mistake. Roma had underestimated Ralph.

As fast as a lightning flash, Ralph came up out of his doubled-over stance. Though his poor physical condition was evident in the whiteness of his face, he unleashed a flurry of blows that drove Roma backwards.

Either Roma was weakening or there was more force in Ralph's punches now. He couldn't tell which. A left jab caught him full in the face, knocking him back against the two horses. Both animals panicked, bumping against Roma and shoving him forward, straight into a crushing blow from Ralph. It caught Roma on the jaw with such force that his mind went blank, then black.

When his head cleared, Roma found himself on his knees. He looked up at Ralph, who stood with his fists raised, waiting for him to get up. For all his sickly looks, Richard Ralph was a natural-born fighter. Though giving his adversary credit, Roma told himself that he had to put an end to their battle. Never having been defeated in a gun- or fist-fight, Roma didn't intend to be humiliated here in the Hallerans' yard.

Coming up on his feet, he feigned unsteadiness. Encouraged by this, Ralph went immediately on the attack. Ready for him, Roma feinted with a deliberately clumsy left-hand punch. Contemptuous of the bigger man's effort, Ralph permitted himself a bleak smile as he slipped in under Roma's left hand. It was a smooth, accomplished move, but it brought Ralph into the trap Roma had planned.

Ralph's face ran straight into a terrific right-hand punch from Roma that lifted him clear off his feet. Arms flailing, Ralph flew backwards through the air until he crashed heavily to the ground on his back. This time there was no instant springing back into action. Stunned, Ralph rose to a half-sitting position. Blood poured from his nose and mouth, and he was making choking noises.

Seeing that Ralph had landed beside his own gunbelt, Roma felt threatened. Ralph's hand was no more than an inch away from the butt of his .45. Roma's horse, with his gun and gunbelt draped across the saddle, having shied, now stood some distance away. Too far for him to reach his Colt before Ralph could cut him down.

But Ralph ignored his .45, and Roma respected him even more. Hand clapped to her mouth, a frightened Queenie watched her husband use a sleeved arm to wipe some of the blood from his face. Ralph came up on one knee. Resting his arms on the raised knee, he laid his head on them. His breathing sounded tortured, and Roma found it difficult to understand how a man could keep going under such a handicap.

Wondering what was to happen next, Roma turned to Queenie, hoping for a clue. He immediately paid the price for taking his eyes off Ralph. There was an explosion inside of Roma's head as a heavy blow caught him under the left eye, widening and lengthening the cut in his cheek. Impossible though it was to believe, the tough Ralph had come up from the ground and was picking Roma off with fast, accurate punches.

Unable to co-ordinate his mind and body under the vicious assault, Roma gave ground. He tried to fend off his assailant with a punch, but his arm felt leaden and Ralph avoided it easily. A left fist knocked Roma's head one way, and a right fist slammed it back the other way, and he fell on his hands and knees, blood dripping into the dust from the cut on his cheek.

Though he hadn't been knocked out, Roma didn't attempt to get up. He signalled with a hand that he'd had enough. Richard Ralph stood swaying, and probably would have fallen had not Hal Halleran hurried to his side. Halleran was holding his bloodied son-in-law upright as Roma struggled to regain his feet. Untying his bandanna, Roma used it to dab at the blood on his face.

Taking a few staggering steps towards the other two men, Roma shakily waved a hand to indicate Ralph to the rancher, saying, 'I'd say you've got yourself a son there, Halleran.'

'I reckon as how you're right, Roma.' A pleased Halleran smiled, turning the steadying arm he had around Ralph's shoulders into a hug.

'And a daughter,' Queenie said softly, going over to stand by her husband and father.

Feeling stronger now, the full use of his legs having returned to him, Roma turned away and walked to his horse. As he reached for the reins, Queenie came to his side to ask a question. 'I have to know, Cado. Could you have beaten Richard?'

'I don't know,' Roma replied truthfully. 'Maybe not. All you need to know, Queenie, is that you've got yourself a real hard man.'

'I'm aware of that,' Queenie said as, without another word or a look, Roma wheeled his horse and headed off in the direction of Minerva Wells.

He pushed his horse at a gallop, but was disappointed when he arrived in town to find that the stage had left. Vern Graff had seen him ride in and walked over to him. Squinting at Roma's battered face, the marshal casually enquired, 'You been kicked by a bull, Cado?'

'It sure feels like it, Vern,' Roma answered. 'Would you believe that Richard Ralph did this to me?'

'After what I've seen today, I'd believe it if you told me Muriel Halleran had roughed you up,' Graff said with a chuckle. 'What brought you back to Minerva Wells, Cado, a pretty little thing by the name of Ruth?'

Shaking his head in wonderment, Roma asked, 'How does a man like you get to know these things, Marshal?'

'Intuition.' The lawman grinned. 'Like I know that we'd better get you down to Holley's livery so's you can buy a horse and saddle. You'll need to ride fast if you're going to catch up with that stage.'

Vern Graff was right. Leading the spare saddled horse, Roma did ride fast. Beside a strong-flowing river, he passed through a narrow gorge to draw abreast with the stage and stop it. There was a slot in the cliff beside them, through which the water of the river was pouring like a vertical white stripe against the grey-brown of the rock.

The bewhiskered man who was riding shotgun used his head to gesture to the empty saddle of the horse Roma was leading, saying wryly, 'If this is a hold-up, young fella, I oughta tell ya that there's just one of ya.'

Looking at the saddle, Roma made a show of

scanning the valley behind him. He muttered, 'Doggone it, what's happened to Luke?'

'I guess if you're not after the strongbox,' the man chuckled, white teeth showing through the gap in his beard, 'there's only one other reason why you're here. She's inside, young fella.'

As Roma was dismounting, Ruth looked out of the window at him. As he walked towards the coach, she alighted and came to him, smiling.

'You can ride with me if you wish, Ruth,' he told her, 'but I don't know where I'm going. It could be any place.'

'It's sure to be better than where I was headed,' she assured him.

'Where were you going?'

'I don't know.'

They laughed together, and as he guided her by the arm to the horse and placed her foot in the stirrup, there was the crack of a whip and the stagecoach creakily moved off. The man riding shotgun waved a hand to them. Roma and Ruth waved back.